CW01510263

M.C. Beaton

with R.W. Green

Agatha Raisin
SUGAR AND SPITE

M.C. Beaton

with R.W. Green

Agatha Raisin
SUGAR AND SPITE

CONSTABLE

CONSTABLE

First published in Great Britain in 2025 by Constable

Copyright © M.C. Beaton Limited 2025

1 3 5 7 9 10 8 6 4 2

A CIP catalogue record for this book
is available from the British Library.

ISBN 978-1-40872-137-7

Typeset in Palatino by Initial Typesetting Services, Edinburgh
Printed and bound in Great Britain by Clays Ltd, Elcograf S.p.A.

Papers used by Constable are from well-managed forests
and other responsible sources

Constable
An imprint of
Little, Brown Book Group
Carmelite House
50 Victoria Embankment
London EC4Y 0DZ

The authorised representative
in the EEA is
Hachette Ireland
8 Castlecourt Centre
Dublin 15, D15 XTP3, Ireland
(email: info@hbgi.ie)

An Hachette UK Company
www.hachette.co.uk

www.littlebrown.co.uk

*For Krystyna – no longer the publisher,
but I'd be lost without you.*

Foreword by R. W. Green

'Sugar and spice and all things nice' is how poet Robert Southey described little girls in a nursery rhyme sometimes known as 'What Are Little Boys Made Of?'. That rhyme is part of a longer poem about what pretty much everyone is made of. But 'Sugar and spice and all things nice' doesn't sound much like Agatha Raisin, does it?

Agatha's a grown woman, not a little girl, but you'd hope that some of the 'all things nice' might have stuck. Well, maybe it didn't stick entirely. Some years ago, when M. C. Beaton (Marion) was talking to me about Agatha, she described her ace detective as being vain, short-tempered, jealous, selfish, demeaning and judgemental . . . but not so much that we'd ever hate her. Her greatest redeeming quality is that, ultimately, she has a heart of gold, and most of her less attractive character traits aren't as horrendously bad as they might be. In fact, they're just bad enough to allow her to say and do things that most of us would never dare. Marion always took great delight in letting Agatha say things she would have liked to say herself. Mind you, Marion wasn't known for holding back. She'd speak her mind when she wanted to, but I know that she, just like most of the rest of us, suffered from the frustration of coming up with exactly what she should have said about an hour after she needed to have said it! Agatha suffers from no such affliction.

In *Sugar and Spite*, Agatha encounters three women whose friendship has turned from spice to spite, and the more she delves into their backgrounds, the more the darker side of their nature is revealed. Like Agatha, the three women are, of course, fictional characters, but some of their circumstances are very real. For example, they defend their 'right to roam' across a farmer's land, which is a contentious issue in the UK, where most areas of countryside are owned by someone. There are areas of public or 'common' land but, in general, if you're out in the countryside, the patch of ground you're standing on belongs to somebody, somewhere.

Public access to privately owned land generally extends to mountains, moors and heathland, and usually excludes using any kind of vehicle. Walkers can hike across the land as long as they do so responsibly, and entering any fields or enclosures where there is livestock or crops under cultivation is usually forbidden.

Naturally, farmers are unhappy about ramblers appearing on their land. Such visitors often bring their dogs, and dogs will chase sheep, causing pregnant ewes to lose their unborn lambs or even die of heart failure, such is the stress caused by a dog – even one who just wants to play. People can also unwittingly spread disease, infecting livestock. Travel restrictions and the closure of public rights of way were imposed when the UK suffered a devastating outbreak of foot-and-mouth disease in 2001.

Almost twenty years prior to the foot-and-mouth disaster, Britain's farmers had to endure the spread of BSE (bovine spongiform encephalopathy), also known as 'mad cow disease', which resulted in the slaughter of four million cattle. It is, therefore, entirely understandable that farmers are reluctant to allow ramblers to go tromping across their land, potentially spreading infections from one farm to another. There probably wouldn't have been any real problem, however, with access to the woods visited by the 'twitchers' in this story.

Twitchers are a real phenomenon, some saying that the term comes from these bird enthusiasts acting like small birds themselves, constantly alert and twitching, ready to race off when any sighting of a rare bird is reported. Unlike other birdwatchers, who will patiently and methodically observe, photograph, record and study their subjects, twitchers want to notch up the greatest number of sightings they possibly can. That's why rumours of a magnolia warbler sighting in the woods prove irresistible to the twitchers in this story – only a handful have ever been recorded in the UK. A magnolia warbler in the Cotswolds would cause huge excitement.

The Cotswolds and the fictional village of Carsely are Agatha's home territory. Unlike her previous adventure in *Killing Time*, when she visited Mallorca, in *Sugar and Spite*, Agatha stays close to home and it's important that she does so. After all, even though it's just a small village tucked away among woodlands, hills and fields, there's always plenty happening in and around Carsely that requires Agatha's detection skills! Carsely is very much part of the cast of characters in any Agatha Raisin tale – another thing that Marion always stressed. Other characters come and go, playing greater or lesser roles in Agatha's adventures, but, no matter where else she travels in the UK or abroad, she will always come home to Carsely.

I hope you enjoy your latest visit to Carsely, too!

R. W. Green, 2025

What are little girls made of?
What are little girls made of?
Sugar and spice
And all things nice
That's what little girls are made of

English poet Robert Southey, *c.*1820

Chapter One

'Twitchers?' Agatha Raisin frowned at her friend Margaret Bloxby, and instantly felt the dreaded wrinkles forming on her forehead and released her eyebrows so quickly she felt her ears twitch. There was that word again – twitch. What on earth were 'twitchers'? She knew she should know. The word seemed familiar but it was filed too far back in her brain to fight its way forward, an intensely annoying state of affairs that had been afflicting her rather too often of late.

Twitchers – the word made her think of the disgustingly large bluebottle she'd seen dying on her kitchen floor earlier that morning. By the time she'd fetched the vacuum cleaner to get rid of it, it had disappeared. Her two cats, Boswell and Hodge, were sitting close to where the unfortunate bluebottle had been, both gazing up at her with wide, innocent eyes. Then Boswell licked his lips and she knew exactly where the bluebottle had gone. She'd returned the vacuum to its home in the little cupboard under the stairs and made a mental note not to stroke Boswell for the rest of the day, wary of witnessing the unsavoury return of a coughed-up, half-chewed, half-dead creature.

Half-dead creatures – that was the other thing 'twitchers' reminded her of. She'd been channel-flicking late one evening, trying to find something interesting to watch on TV, when she'd accidentally come across a zombie movie in which twitching, drooling, reanimated corpses were stumbling around only to be re-killed in the most gory, gruesome ways imaginable. Agatha had switched off the TV and instead curled up with a much-thumbed copy of The Detection Club's *The Floating Admiral* accompanied by a large glass of Primitivo.

'Yes, twitchers,' Margaret replied. 'At the Carsely Ladies Society meeting in the church hall this evening.'

That probably ruled out zombies. Agatha had attended many meetings of the Ladies Society, including a lecture on Capability Brown's Cotswold landscapes, which she'd quite enjoyed, and one on the history of needlepoint, which she hadn't. She'd once even given a talk to the combined ranks of the Carsely and Ancombe societies. While she'd seen a few of the most elderly attendees nod off for a bit and come dribbling back to life, she'd never witnessed anyone actually snuff it, return from the dead and lurch around the room twitching. Not that anyone had fallen asleep during her talk, of course. They'd all been fascinated by her stories about running her own private detective agency, Raisin Investigations. She knew that her tales of skulduggery, infidelity and murder, with the perpetrators' names discreetly omitted, had given her unusually attentive audience weeks of delicious gossip over tea and custard creams as they speculated about the indentities of the swindlers, adulterers and killers. Not your average zombies, then.

'Twitchers are birdwatchers, Agatha,' Margaret explained, recognising the mildly perplexed look creeping onto her friend's face despite Agatha's attempts to disguise it. 'I think the ones who take it most seriously should properly be called "birders", but twitchers is the term that's caught on.'

'Yes, yes ... I know that,' Agatha said, nodding. It wasn't a lie. Now that Margaret had told her, she most certainly *did* know. In fact, she'd known all along. She'd even posed as a twitcher not so long ago when she and her friend Roy Silver were checking out the grounds of an old mansion that belonged to a murder suspect. Having let the word slip her mind irritated her, and the fact that it wasn't the first time it had happened recently was really beginning to annoy her, although she was determined not to let her temper get the better of her in front of Margaret. 'I was only wondering whether it might be of any interest, really.'

Agatha took a sip of sherry from a crystal schooner then set it carefully back down in front of her. They were sitting in Margaret's garden at a small, round, ornately moulded, white-painted metal table. Their white metal chairs were fashioned to the same design and Agatha was beginning to wish they had cushions. She was wearing a thin summer dress and could feel the chair's swirling leaf motif slowly pressing its pattern into her buttocks. She shifted slightly to relieve the pressure and was dismayed when she immediately felt everything settle back into the same position.

The mild discomfort was easy to ignore when she took a moment to appreciate her surroundings. Margaret was married to Alf Bloxby, vicar to the Church of St Jude in

Carsely, and this corner of the vicarage garden, a small patio just outside the kitchen door, was a real suntrap. They were sitting with their backs to a high stone wall that was all but invisible, shrouded in the dark green leaves of a clematis festooned with purple blooms as big as the span of Agatha's hand. Flouncing frills of pink and orange trailing begonias tumbled from hanging baskets, while geraniums in pots and planters stretched perfectly round heads of red, white and pink blooms towards the sun. The air smelled sweet, the sherry was nicely chilled and, all in all, there were worse places to be on a late Friday afternoon.

'Of course it will be of interest,' Margaret assured her. 'You're always telling me that in your line of work you have to take an interest in all sorts of things to make sure you never miss a scrap of evidence, or to give you the best chance of being able to tell when someone's lying to you.'

'That's true,' Agatha agreed. She tapped her temple. 'You store away an awful lot of information in here without even realising it's there or knowing when you might need it. Then, when you *do* actually need it, it just sort of pops to the front of your head.'

Twitchers hadn't, but most things still did.

'You're lucky,' Margaret said, smiling. 'My memory's appalling. I've had to put my glasses on a string round my neck because I kept forgetting where I'd put them.' She plucked at the string to illustrate her point. 'And lately, I've found myself walking upstairs or into a room and I don't have a clue why I went there. Not all of us have the sort of recall that's made you so good at your job.'

'Being a private detective is generally more about mundane hard work than flashes of inspiration,' Agatha said. 'It's about ploughing through paperwork or staring at a computer screen to do background checks. It's about sitting for hours in a car on a surveillance job, or spending forever on the phone trying to track down a missing person.'

'That, I believe, is the sort of perseverance that makes a good twitcher!' Margaret said, with what sounded suspiciously like a note of triumph. Agatha felt as though she'd played straight into her friend's hands and Margaret pressed home her advantage. 'You really should come along tonight, unless you're out dancing again?'

Margaret's gentle smile made it seem almost like she was teasing, something that Agatha tolerated from only two people and, if they were honest, neither of the two could ever be entirely sure they'd get away with it. Margaret was one of the daring duo of brave souls confident enough in their relationships with Agatha to risk suffering the full fury of the infamous Raisin temper. John Glass, a former detective inspector with Mircester Police, was the other.

'John's at a meeting in Southampton,' Agatha explained. 'He won't get back to his place until late, so I won't see him until tomorrow evening.'

'How are things with you two? Is he still sweeping you round the dance floor and whisking you off to bed?'

'Margaret!' Agatha felt her frown returning. 'I don't think that's the sort of question a respectable vicar's wife should be asking!'

'I'll take that as a yes, then!' Margaret said, laughing. 'Don't look so appalled, Agatha. We know each other far better than that. What's John up to in Southampton? Not planning on sailing the high seas again, is he?'

'Maybe,' Agatha said, standing and stepping off to one side. She craned her neck to see out across the garden. 'Is that a woodpecker on the grass?'

When Margaret turned to look for the bird, Agatha vigorously massaged her buttocks through her dress to dispel the leaf imprint.

'Might have been,' Margaret said. 'There's one pays us a visit now and again to pick bugs out of the lawn. You see, you *are* interested in birds! But don't change the subject. Is your dancing policeman off on his travels again?'

'Probably,' Agatha said, with a heavy sigh. 'He's talking it through with the people from the cruise line he used to work for. I thought he'd got that wanderlust out of his system but I was with him when he took the call from them. They asked him to sign on as their dance instructor for a two-week trip to the Norwegian fjords. I saw the way his eyes lit up. Then he looked at me and all that sparkle faded.'

Agatha gently lowered herself back into the seat, trying to get the pattern in a different place. She failed.

'He knew you didn't want him to go.'

'Of course he knew. He didn't spend all those years as a police detective without learning how to read people. He knew I wasn't happy about him going away again, but I told him he should go anyway. He spent years working as a policeman, which isn't the most glamorous job, and now he deserves to be spending his time doing

6

something that makes him happy. I'd have to be a real hard-hearted, miserable cow to deny him that.'

'That's not who you are.'

'Not everyone would agree with you,' Agatha said, standing once more to pace the patio. 'The thing is, in my head part of me is screaming that if he wants to go off dancing on some boat rather than being with me, then he can go to hell and good riddance to him! If he's not happy with me, then I don't want him around!

'On the other hand, I really do want him to be happy and I know I'm going to miss him and I can't stand the thought that I'll be missing him, worrying about him, thinking about him constantly!' She raised her arms wide, then let them drop, her hands slapping her thighs in exasperation. 'He's only been gone a day and I know I'll see him tomorrow, but he's in my mind all the time. It's scrambling my brain! What the hell is wrong with me?'

'I'm not a doctor, Agatha, but I've seen these symptoms before. This is what happens when someone's in love. You've fallen head over heels in love with John Glass!'

'Oh, don't be ridiculous!' Agatha snapped. 'I'm not some silly teenager with a crush on the boy with the dark eyes and wavy hair who works in the butcher's shop!'

'That really happened, didn't it?'

'Never you mind! I'm a grown woman. I've had lots of relationships with lots of men and . . .'

'Well, as a respectable vicar's wife, I—' Margaret began, with a mischievous expression that was immediately dispelled by the look in Agatha's bear-like eyes that simply said, *Don't push it.*

7

'. . . I don't want to feel like this,' Agatha went on. 'I need to be able to think straight. I need to be . . . in control.'

Agatha sat down again, arranging herself sideways, across the pattern.

'What you really need to do is to enjoy every moment you spend with John,' Margaret advised, 'and fill the time you're apart with things that make you think of anything other than the fact he's not there. I take it you're not too busy at work right now?'

'Busy enough,' Agatha said. 'We have regular requests from a number of businesses for background checks on potential employees, there are always law firms asking us to gather evidence in civil cases and the usual surveillance jobs for divorce cases, but they're all things my team can handle with a little organisation and direction. I like to stay on top of everything, but there's nothing too challenging on the books right now.'

'No major crimes for you to get your teeth into . . . no murders.'

'I don't go out looking for that sort of thing, you know. They just seem to land at my feet.'

'Well, if there's nothing like that at your feet right now, what you should do is find something else to occupy your mind – something different. So how about the twitchers' lecture this evening? I can promise you a glass of wine once it's all over.'

'Very well, Mrs Bloxby,' Agatha said slowly, resigning herself to an evening in the church hall. She used the form of address preferred by the Ladies Society. The first-name terms she and Margaret used in private would be a dreadful breach of decorum in public for Carsley's finest – most improper.

'Jolly good, Mrs Raisin,' Margaret replied, holding out her glass. 'Here's to an edifying experience with the twitchers this evening.'

They clinked glasses, finished their drinks and, when they stood to leave the garden, Margaret winced before using both hands to rub her backside.

'I really must make cushions for those chairs,' she said.

Just beyond the outskirts of Mircester, on the road to Carsely, so well hidden in a shallow hollow behind roadside trees and hedges that anyone driving past would hardly notice they were there, stood a small development of modern bungalows called Tweeting Bottom. These were not the kind of mellow Cotswold stone cottages for which the area is famous, but neat, brick-built houses under tiled roofs, sitting behind tidy front lawns. Sensible cars were parked in the short drive-ways adjacent to the lawns, but never on the road that circled the central green. The green itself was like a small meadow, where a variety of grasses thrived alongside white flowerheads of wild carrot, delicate petals of sticky mouse-ear and the sunny yellow blossoms of meadow buttercups and lady's bedstraw.

No one who ever actually spotted the turn-off to the cul-de-sac and ventured in, either out of curiosity or by mistake, lingered longer than it took to loop the green and drive straight back out again. They quickly developed the uncomfortable, creepy feeling they were being watched, and they were right. Unseen eyes observed vigilantly from behind startlingly white net curtains, noting every delivery, tradesman or visitor, so keen were the residents to preserve the tranquil sanctity of Tweeting Bottom and guard against unwelcome interlopers.

The guardians of the Bottom were undoubtedly watching when three ladies, all somewhere in their sixties, gathered beside a large, black car parked obtrusively on the road outside number 12 – Miss Feldrake's house. One of the women was a head taller than the other two, with curly black hair and a generous figure that stretched her tweed jacket and skirt enough to test the quality of the robust tailoring. The second was of slimmer build, with long, grey hair pulled back in a ponytail, a pleasant, round face and dark eyes. She was dressed in jeans and a dark blue cotton jacket over a simple white T-shirt. The last of the three was similar in build to the woman in the blue jacket but had brown, shoulder-length hair, a long, elegant nose and a mouth that seemed a little too low on her chin. She wore walking shorts and a military-style waistcoat with many pockets. This was Joan Feldrake.

'You're not seriously bringing all that stuff, are you?' Stella Smart, the tweedy woman, scowled at the collection of black holdalls accumulating by the tailgate of her car. Feldrake returned the scowl, having expected some sort of comment.

'Yes, I am!' she responded vigorously. 'We will need the projector screen and its stand as well as the projector and its stand if we are to show the audience photos of all the birds you claim to know so much about.' She reached down to pick up what looked like a small briefcase. 'We need my laptop to send the photos to the projector; then there are the cameras, tripods, lenses—'

'Must you really show off that ridiculous long lens?' Smart interrupted. 'You can hardly lift a camera with that attached.'

'I get great results with that lens!' argued Feldrake.

'When you tried to photograph that corncrake last week, you got five shots of the ground and two of an empty branch after the bird had, quite literally, flown.'

'Utter nonsense! I doubt the bird was even there. No one actually saw it except you. They're extremely rare around here, and you wouldn't know a corncrake from a cornflake!'

'Does it really matter how much stuff Joan wants to bring?' asked the third woman, with a plaintive sigh. Mary Carstairs had heard her friends bicker like this more times than she cared to remember. 'You bought a new car the size of a funeral barge, Stella. It's not as if you don't have room.'

'Yes, *I* bought the car, Mary!' Smart snapped. 'You two couldn't whistle up enough cash to buy a bus ticket between you!'

'Neither of us was lucky enough to be left a fortune by an aunt we barely knew!' Feldrake replied.

'I ran a successful business for years and—' Smart said, stabbing a finger in Feldrake's direction to make her point before being cut off.

'For goodness' sake, let's just load up and get going,' Carstairs said, 'otherwise we'll run out of time for setting up in the hall.'

Smart pressed a button on her key fob and the tailgate

rose automatically. She then strutted round to the driver's door, climbing behind the wheel and leaving the others to load the gear. Feldrake and Carstairs lifted the bags into the car then jumped back as Smart promptly closed the tailgate at the flick of a switch without leaving her seat. Feldrake took the passenger seat and Carstairs sat in the back. Silence reigned on the short drive to Carsely, especially after Feldrake reached forward to switch on the radio only to have her hand slapped away by Smart.

They turned off the main road onto the route that took them downhill into the dappled shade of an avenue of trees, arriving in the village of Carsely a few minutes later. They had almost reached St Jude's Church Hall when Carstairs spotted a woman walking up the garden path to the vicarage. She was sure she recognised her. The woman had a glossy bob of brown hair and was wearing a green, leaf-patterned silk blouse with white trousers that draped over her white high heels, contriving to make her legs seem longer than they really were.

'Who's that?' Carstairs piped up. 'Don't we know her?'

'The one in the bloody awful blouse?' asked Smart.

'Yes, Stella,' said Feldrake snidely. 'Since she's the only other person in sight, I'd say that's who we're supposed to be looking at.'

Smart shot Feldrake a sharp look and curled her lip.

'That's Agatha Raisin,' Carstairs said, clapping her hands together as if to congratulate herself on matching the face to a name. 'You know – the detective! I wonder if she's coming to our talk tonight.'

12

'Seems a bit overdressed for a church hall in Carsely,' Smart said, sniffing. 'An old hen in fancy chic feathers.'

'Better plumage than you could ever get away with,' Feldrake said, laughing.

'Please stop bickering, you two,' Carstairs pleaded. 'Let's just concentrate on this evening's talk so it all goes smoothly. We can't do that if we're at each other's throats constantly!'

Agatha approached the vicarage door carrying her handbag over her arm along with a pashmina of rich, dark green trimmed with delicate gold embroidery in a pattern of swirling leaves. The evening was still warm, having even grown rather humid, but she knew from experience that the old church hall could be chilly, so having the shawl to drape over her shoulders seemed prudent. She noticed the large black car pulling up outside the hall. She was a little too early for the Ladies Society talk and assumed that, since the car was also early, it was probably the twitchers. Two of the car's three occupants began unloading various items, supervised by the third.

Agatha made to grasp the door knocker and paused. Despite having clunked the brass ring against the old wooden door's striking plate on countless previous visits, she realised for the first time that it was held in the mouth of a placid, yet powerful-looking lion. Having noticed the lion, she now became captivated by it. The lion's head looked far more noble than either of her two cats could ever manage, but just as she reached out a finger to stroke its nose, the door was flung open and she found herself pointing straight into the face of the Reverend Alfred Bloxby. He jumped back, spluttering in surprise.

'Mrs Raisin ... I ... I ...' he stammered. Agatha knew that Margaret's husband didn't approve of their friendship, believing her to be an unhealthy influence on his wife. He had a point. Agatha and Margaret had found themselves in some tricky situations together, once even facing up to a gunman. And who could forget when Margaret had almost died, accidentally shot with an arrow intended for Agatha? It was little wonder the vicar referred to Agatha as 'that dreadful woman', and hardly a shock to her when she inevitably found out he did so. Listening to loose talk was part of her business, and gossip had a way of finding her ear, often lured with a cash reward. Yet, no matter what he said about her, Agatha could hardly treat Alf Bloxby as she would any other adversary. A blast of her ferocious temper or a smack in the mouth would not be appropriate. He was a vicar, after all, and, even more importantly, Margaret's husband. He meant the world to Margaret, so Agatha always tried her best to waltz carefully around the vicar, wearing her softest, most diplomatic dancing shoes. She was, however, a far better dancer than diplomat.

'I was admiring the lion's head,' she said, lowering her finger like a gunslinger holstering his six-shooter, determined to try to make polite conversation no matter how awkward it might feel. 'It ... um ... seems a little odd for someone like you – a gentle, peace-loving Christian, I mean – to have such a ferocious creature on the front door.'

'Not at all,' he replied, composing himself. 'Several of the saints are associated with lions, including Daniel, of course, and Jesus was known as the Lion of Judah and ... but ... but I really must get on. I was just leaving and I'm in rather a hurry.'

Clearly, the vicar found the encounter every bit as uncomfortable as she did, and with that, he scurried off towards his car. Margaret then appeared in the vicarage doorway.

'I see you bumped into Alf,' she said.

'I almost poked him in the eye,' Agatha explained.

'Oh dear! Was it something he said?'

'No, he didn't ... I was just about to ...' Agatha waved her hand as if to erase her explanation and pointed towards the black car outside the church hall. 'He was fine. I think the twitchers have arrived.'

The two friends made their way towards the church hall, where Feldrake and Carstairs were carrying bags inside while Smart held the door open. By the time they caught up with the three women, they were unpacking equipment on the small stage at the front of the hall.

Margaret introduced Agatha and Carstairs stepped forward to shake hands, but Smart pushed in front of her, grasping Agatha's hand in a crushing grip.

'So happy to see you here, Mrs Raisin,' she said, brimming with false geniality. 'We had no idea you were interested in birds.'

'Oh, I'm interested in all sorts of things,' Agatha replied, retrieving her hand and flexing her fingers.

'Some of your equipment, for example, looks very familiar.'

'Yes, I never go anywhere without these,' Smart said, holding up a very large pair of binoculars in her left hand, putting them to her eyes and aiming at the exposed roof beams. 'Rather a lot of cobwebs up there, Mrs Bloxby.'

'Yes, I've used binoculars many times,' Agatha said, then pointed to a smaller device Feldrake had just unzipped from its case, 'but I've never seen one of those before. What is that, Miss Feldrake?'

'It's a monocular,' Feldrake explained. 'Binoculars can be a bit unwieldy, particularly if you're also carrying a camera with a long lens.'

'Those can be very cumbersome,' Agatha agreed, 'especially if you're trying to shoot from a car, as I often am.'

'The monocular is light and compact,' Feldrake said, handing it to Agatha. 'It gives good magnification and you can even clip your phone to it to grab photos you might otherwise miss.'

'Really? I've used a little telescope in the past but this is way better. I must get one of these.' Agatha scanned the room but stopped when Smart appeared in the eye-piece, blurred from her close proximity.

'Well, I'm sticking with the binoculars,' Smart said with a smug smile. 'I've spotted more different species of birds with these than anyone else in the whole of the Cotswolds.'

'So you say,' Carstairs said quietly, 'but we've only your word for most of those sightings, haven't we?'

Smart turned to Carstairs with a flash of anger in her

16

eyes but Margaret intervened before another word could be said.

'How about some tea?' she offered. 'Can I tempt you with a strawberry tart as well, or would you prefer to wait until the ladies begin to arrive? They're all far better bakers than me and they always bring the most delicious cakes.'

Margaret led them past the rows of folding chairs she had laid out earlier that day to where a long table, resplendent in a gleaming white cloth, proudly displayed dozens of white cups with saucers, three multi-tiered cake stands crammed with strawberry tarts, jugs of milk, boxes of tea bags and a tall, stainless-steel hot-water urn.

Agatha draped her pashmina over her shoulders and followed the twitchers, listening to them hiss at each other under their breath. She didn't need her detective's observational skills or even a twinkle of inspiration to recognise the atmosphere of animosity between the three. Never mind the lecture on watching birds, watching the lecturers snipe at each other every chance they got promised to make this a hugely entertaining evening.

Agatha accepted a cup of tea but declined a strawberry tart. Hungry though she was, and as delicious as the tarts looked, her white trousers and the gooey deliciousness of the tart filling, some of which she could see forming a creeping red dribble at the corner of Miss Smart's mouth, were a recipe for disaster. Yet the tarts were seriously tempting. She distracted herself by observing the members of the Carsely Ladies Society beginning to drift into the hall. Some wore pale blue or pink cardigans, some wore loose summer tops, some wore both. Rain was forecast, although not until tomorrow afternoon, yet there were older women taking no chances in light summer raincoats that reached to just above the knee and buttoned all the way down the front, making them look like school dinner ladies from a bygone era, which they might well have been. Some of the slightly more daring, slightly younger women sported short rain jackets that scarcely reached below their hips. There were a few familiar faces but none Agatha knew particularly well.

They all greeted each other politely and made lively conversation about children, grandchildren and the scandal of the day – the fact that the man with the fish van hadn't appeared in the village that afternoon as he normally did. Tinned salmon just wasn't the same, was it? Agatha heard one woman describe how her husband had come home from work only to be told she couldn't give him his usual Friday-night home-made fish and chips because she hadn't had time to get to the supermarket for cod fillets. He had stormed off to the Red Lion, and the slight alcohol-induced flush in her cheeks was evidence that she had followed the storm to join him there.

Sponges, muffins and scones appeared on the table alongside the cake stands, Margaret producing a stack of paper plates and plastic forks. More ladies than Agatha had ever seen at a society meeting filed in, many immediately recognising her, and she was obliged to field a barrage of questions that ranged from 'Does a lost cat count as a missing person?' and 'How can I find out how much my husband squanders in the Red Lion?' to 'Do you think the fish man's been murdered?' Then she

18

finally spotted a face she recognised – Doris Simpson, her cleaning lady.

'Hello, Mrs Raisin,' Doris said cheerfully. 'Fancy meeting you here!'

'I could say the same,' Agatha said, 'but it's so nice to see a friendly face. I didn't know you were interested in birdwatching.'

'I'm not,' Doris said, smoothing her white hair and patting its bun while leaning in close to whisper, 'and neither's most of the others here tonight.'

'Really?' Agatha said, also lowering her voice despite the din of chatter echoing around the hall. 'Why is there such a good turnout then?'

'They've not come to hear about birds,' Doris chuckled. 'They've come to catch up on all the best gossip and to see if those three,' she pointed subtly towards the three twitchers now joining Margaret on the stage, 'can get through the evening without having an almighty row!'

'I can believe that,' Agatha agreed. 'They were snarling at each other like angry cats earlier. Hardly the best of friends.'

'Oh, but that's the funniest thing of all, Mrs Raisin!' Doris laughed. 'They *are* the best of friends – have been since they were at school!'

Doris bustled off for a tea refill and a strawberry tart as the ladies took their seats. Agatha sat in the back row, where none of the seats had been taken, in order to avoid attracting any more attention, and Margaret took centre stage to introduce Miss Smart, Miss Feldrake and Miss Carstairs.

19

'This evening, I will be telling you about some of the many, many different species of birds I have observed,' Smart said, taking over from Margaret. 'I've most certainly spotted more birds than anyone in . . .'

'Her imagination,' Feldrake said in a loud stage whisper, rolling her eyes. Smart glowered at her and Carstairs raised a hand to cover a smile.

'. . . than anyone in the region,' Smart went on. 'Miss Carstairs will explain a little about where you can best spot different types of birds in the local area, and Miss Feldrake has taken a few snaps to try to show what we're talking about. Sorry if they're a bit fuzzy . . .'

Margaret dimmed the lights and Carstairs stepped forward to explain about what to look for in different environments of open fields, meadows, wetlands and woodlands around Carsely. Agatha felt her tummy rumble and finally gave in to the temptation of the strawberry tarts, taking advantage of the lights going down to dart across to the table to grab a tart on a paper plate. She had just settled back into her seat and lifted the tart to her mouth, about to take a bite, when she heard what she thought was the hall door closing. She looked round and saw the merest whisper of movement in the shadows by the cloakroom. Lowering the tart carefully back onto its plate, she parked it on the seat next to her and stared into the cloakroom's murky recess, but could see nothing. Maybe her imagination was playing tricks on her. She switched her focus back to the stage.

'This photograph,' Carstairs said, motioning Feldrake to change the photo showing on the screen, 'was taken just a few days ago—'

'On my land!' boomed a voice from the back of the hall. Agatha, along with most of the Carsely Ladies, turned to see a tall man step out of the shadows by the cloakroom. Margaret reacted instantly, reaching for the light switches. All the hall lights flickered into life, as did a few of the ladies dozing in the audience. The man had the dark, lined skin of someone who had spent a lifetime working outdoors and a shaggy crop of black hair. He looked, Agatha guessed, to be in his early fifties and was ruggedly handsome. He pointed to the screen, and then to the three women on stage.

'You've been trespassing again!' he growled. 'I already told you lot not to go tromping over my fields! Well, I won't tell you again! If I catch any of you anywhere on my land in future, you're for it!'

'For what, exactly?' Smart said, squaring her substantial shoulders and glaring out at him from the stage. 'We have a right to roam – it's the law! You can't own the countryside. It's for everyone to enjoy!'

'You've no right to roam over my land!' The growl turned to a roar. 'Stay away, or you'll regret it!'

'And what are you going to do?' Feldrake stood at Smart's shoulder. 'Blast us with your shotgun? We're not helpless little creatures, you know. We're not like all the rabbits, pigeons and pheasants you shoot!'

'Joan's right!' yelled Carstairs, stepping forward to stand with her friends and shaking her fist. 'You can't just mow us down like you do those poor birds. We won't stand for it! We can look after ourselves!'

Agatha admired the way the three women had suddenly gone from squabbling like teenagers to standing

21

firm together. They looked like a slightly greying squad of vigilante pensioners. The heads in the audience were turning in unison from the stage to the angry man and back again, as if watching an ill-tempered tennis match. If they'd come hoping for an entertaining quarrel, they wouldn't be disappointed, and they seemed as impressed with the twitchers' response as Agatha was. The man at the back of the hall, however, was completely unperturbed.

'Is that so?' he said. His voice was now quiet, yet filled the room with a menace that rumbled like distant thunder. 'You people are a disease. Final warning. Set foot on my land again and I'll exterminate you like vermin!'

He turned, flung open the hall's heavy oak door as though brushing aside a wind-blown leaf and strode out into the fading evening light. A still hush descended over the hall. Agatha rose from her seat, trotting over to the door to take another look at the man, but caught no more than a glimpse of him disappearing behind some parked cars further up the high street. She closed the door and sat down again, immediately feeling a strange sensation. Then every muscle in her body froze.

'More tea, anyone?' Margaret asked with forced merriment, walking past the rows of silent ladies towards Agatha. 'Do, please, help yourselves, then we can get back to our talk.'

A murmur of conversation swiftly swelled to a clamour that filled the room, the Carsely Ladies Society finding its voice again, quickly establishing from those in the know exactly who the man had been and then circulating dark yarns about his past misdemeanours. By the time they all crowded round the refreshments table, the most contemptible stories had evolved into truly abominable tales and even more salacious, probably slanderous, accounts were being discussed. He was a farmer, but he lived alone on his isolated farm. Why was he trying to keep people away? What did he get up to out there where no one could see him? What secrets was he hiding?

'Mrs Raisin,' Margaret said, approaching Agatha with a look of concern and crouching beside her, 'you look a little out of sorts. Is everything all right?'

'Help me, Margaret!' Agatha whispered desperately. 'I can't move!'

Chapter Two

'Whatever's the matter?' Margaret asked, crouching beside Agatha and reaching out to hold her hand. 'What's happened to you?'

'I can't move,' Agatha repeated, a look of panic in her eyes. 'I need your help. I don't know what to say. I . . . I've sat on a strawberry tart!'

Showing levels of restraint, self-control and Christian charity bordering on miraculous, the vicar's wife displayed not even the hint of a smile, maintaining an expression of grave concern as she rose slowly to her feet.

'I see,' she said solemnly. 'White trousers – strawberry tart. That's not going to look good, is it? Stay where you are and try to act normal. I'll bring you a cup of tea and work out what to do.'

Some of the Carsely Ladies may have wondered why, as she manoeuvred her way through the crowd to reach the tea table, Mrs Bloxby appeared to be giggling, especially when they were discussing the serious issue of why their recently departed, very angry, male visitor was so intent on keeping people away from his farm. What was his secret? He seemed violent enough to be

24

a killer, perhaps even a serial killer! Were there bodies buried in his fields? On the other hand, was he perhaps wanted by the authorities for something else? Maybe he was an international fugitive – a war criminal wanted for atrocities carried out in some faraway conflict! The tastiest morsel of speculation came from two of the most enthusiastic gossips, who each claimed to have heard he was some kind of mad scientist conducting bizarre experiments in a clandestine laboratory in his barn.

With no evidence to support any of their theories, the most outrageous trumped all others and the man was tagged as a modern-day Frankenstein. Those few who quietly professed to know the sad truth were simply shouted down, their opinions dismissed, their theories far too banal. Agatha listened from a distance, pretending to take an urgent call on her mobile as an excuse to remain apart from the others. One or two of the ladies gave her a curious look, but most were absorbed in their verbal annihilation of the male intruder. By the time Margaret returned with a cup of tea for Agatha, her staid expression restored, she'd worked out how to deal with the strawberry tart disaster.

'I'd put that away,' she said, indicating the phone in Agatha's hand. 'Everyone knows there's no phone reception in here. Now, all you have to do is sit tight. In a couple of minutes, I'll get the twitchers back on stage and the ladies back in their seats. Then, once I've turned the lights down, I'll pop round to the vicarage. I've a green, wrap-around skirt that should fit you and will suit your blouse. You can sneak off to change in the loo at the back of the hall.'

25

Agatha looked up at her friend and, her shoulders relaxing in relief, said simply, 'Thank you.'

When the twitchers eventually finished their presentation, the Carsely Ladies filtered out of the hall as quickly as they could shuffle through the door. Most were desperate to get home before the evening grew too late. There were people to call. Some had mobile phones in their hands even before they hit the street, and Agatha was sure that the phone lines out of Carsely would be buzzing with intrigue for hours to come. It's not every meeting of the Carsely Ladies Society, after all, that's interrupted by a man who, by the time the delicious gossip had snowballed to avalanche proportions, is probably wanted by Interpol, MI6 and the CIA.

Agatha's switch from trousers to skirt had gone smoothly, even if the skirt was a little tight in the waist, and she was pleased that Margaret had been absolutely right about the colour. It wasn't something she would have chosen for herself, but she was prepared to compromise in an emergency. She lingered as she followed Margaret past the refreshments table, eyeing the mountain of dirty cups.

'Don't worry about those,' Margaret said. 'I'll bung them all in the dishwasher later. The junior badminton club will be using the hall tomorrow morning and they'll clear the chairs away – as well as any leftover cake I leave out for them! How are the trousers? You know, you might be able to rescue them with—'

'Thanks, Margaret, but I don't wear rescued clothes,'

Agatha said. 'I'd rather forget about the trousers, so I've binned them. Let's see how the twitchers are getting along.'

It immediately became clear that the twitchers were not getting along at all well. A blazing row had erupted and sparks were flying as Agatha and Margaret approached the stage.

'You should have told us you were going there!' Smart snarled at Feldrake, while watching her and Carstairs pack away the gear.

'Why should I tell you everything I do?' demanded Feldrake. 'I can go wherever I like, and you can't stop me! What I do is none of your business!'

'But it is our business if you go trespassing and get us into trouble,' Carstairs pointed out. 'That man is a bully and we can't afford to hand him ammunition to use against us!'

'I didn't give him . . .' Feldrake paused when she realised Agatha and Margaret had joined them.

'That was a fascinating talk, ladies,' Margaret congratulated them, 'despite the little intrusion.'

'Yes, you did well to pick up the pieces after that man caused such a rumpus,' Agatha agreed. 'Who was he?'

'Guy Fawkes,' Carstairs said, looking at Agatha's skirt with an expression of mild confusion.

'Guy Fawkes?' Agatha raised an eyebrow. 'Same as the man who tried to blow up the Houses of Parliament all those centuries ago?'

'Same name,' Smart said, waving a hand as though dismissing any further thought of the man, 'but he's a nobody. We've had run-ins with him before.'

'So he said,' Agatha pointed out, 'and tonight he sounded deadly serious. He made a very clear threat against all three of you.'

'Oh, we're not worried about that silly man, Mrs Raisin,' Smart said, with a short laugh. 'We can handle him. Come along now, girls. Let's get this stuff out to the car.'

Carstairs and Feldrake gathered up the bags – politely refusing any help from Agatha or Margaret – then the twitchers loaded their equipment and themselves into Smart's car and were gone. Having waved them off, Margaret led Agatha back to the vicarage for the previously promised glass of wine.

'That turned out to be a far more turbulent evening than I'd imagined,' Agatha said, sinking into the feather cushions on one of the welcoming armchairs by the fireplace in Margaret's sitting room. There were few other places, apart from her own cottage in Lilac Lane, where Agatha felt quite so comfortable. The room had the aroma of lavender and furniture polish with a sweet, lingering hint of woodsmoke which, Agatha assumed, must have permeated everything in the room given that the fire hadn't been lit all summer.

'Well, it's not every evening you have such a traumatic wardrobe disaster involving a strawberry tart,' Margaret replied, handing Agatha a glass of Merlot. She settled into the other armchair by the fireplace after stooping for a moment to reposition one of the blooms in a flower display arranged in a large vase standing on the hearth, cheering up the empty grate.

'I didn't mean that,' Agatha said, almost as if she'd

already forgotten the incident. 'I meant the man who burst in and threatened the twitchers – Guy Fawkes.'

'I don't think that's his real name,' Margaret said. 'His surname is definitely Fawkes but I'm sure everyone with that name gets called "Guy", whether it's their actual name or not.'

'You don't know him, then?'

'Not really. I know he has a farm somewhere on the edge of the Barfield Estate and that his wife died a few years ago, but that's about it.'

'Did Alf handle the funeral?'

'No, we didn't have anything to do with that. I believe Mr Fawkes and his wife both had family roots in Wales. I remember her name was Rhiannon – I've always thought that such a lovely name. The funeral was somewhere in Wales. Alf reached out to him at the time, but he didn't seem to need any help from us. He's fiercely independent.'

'He's certainly fierce. That was quite a display of temper.'

'There are always reasons why people behave the way they do,' Margaret said, pausing for a moment to take a sip of wine. 'No doubt there's a deeper unhappiness that stokes his anger.'

'No doubt,' Agatha agreed, 'but he also has a flair for drama. His departure this evening was like something from a Brontë novel.'

'You're right!' Margaret laughed. 'He had a touch of Jane Eyre's Mr Rochester!'

'Not quite the aristocrat that Rochester was,' Agatha mused, 'but an interesting character nonetheless.'

'My goodness, how long ago was it ...?' Margaret said, stroking her chin as if to conjure up a memory. 'I haven't read *Jane Eyre* since I was twelve. I remember . . .'

The conversation quickly spiralled away from the events of that evening, but Agatha was left with a powerful image of the dark and brooding Mr Fawkes crashing in and out of her head. Try as she might to banish him, to lock her mind's door and keep him out, he just kept flinging it open again. In the end, she realised she'd rather he stayed. There was something that intrigued her about Mr Fawkes and she knew she wouldn't be able to push him out of her thoughts until she'd found out more about him.

Agatha was woken before dawn by what sounded like handfuls of gravel being flung at her bedroom window. She drew back the curtains and looked out on a raging storm. The flowers in her front garden and the beautiful lilacs in neighbouring gardens, from which Lilac Lane took its name, had lost their vibrant colours in the flat streetlight, but were whipping back and forth with the howling gale threatening to flatten them completely. She stepped back when the wind splattered another barrage of raindrops against the window. It looked like a different world from the tranquil summer's evening Carsely had enjoyed just a few hours ago. Tranquil, that is, apart from the events at the church hall.

She pulled the curtains and climbed back into bed, noting that both cats were sleeping at the bottom of her duvet, utterly undisturbed by the storm. As she drifted off to sleep once more, the mysterious Mr Fawkes flashed into her mind. He was setting fire to a large building . . . not the Houses of Parliament, but Thornfield Hall, where Mr Rochester lived in *Jane Eyre*. The building was ablaze, just as happened in the novel, and someone who looked a lot like John was busy rescuing servants and cats from the inferno. Then Agatha felt herself falling, tumbling from the battlements, just like Rochester's wife. She felt the heat as she plummeted past the flames but surprised herself by appearing to enjoy the fall. Strangely, there was no fear or dread of her impending, presumably painful and undoubtedly terminal contact with the ground. Then she was suddenly safe, caught and held in the strong arms of Fawkes.

Agatha woke with a start, gasping as if she'd had the breath knocked out of her and almost convinced she could feel Fawkes's arms around her. She sat up in bed and, in the dim light filtering through the curtains, saw Boswell and Hodge staring at her.

'What the hell was all that about?' she asked, although neither cat offered an answer. 'What did it mean? I know, I know . . . dreams don't really mean anything. They're just your mind having fun on its rest break. There's nothing to see here. Just go back to sleep.'

The cats did exactly that, and so did she.

Later that day, Joan Feldrake was sitting at her kitchen table in Tweeting Bottom, sipping coffee and editing photographs on her laptop. She glanced out of the window at the silver birch tree in her garden, its branches waving wildly in the wind. The rain had eased, the gale having chased it north-east to Coventry and Leicester, and the sky was brightening, but the wind was still scouring the Cotswolds.

Feldrake had spent most of the day sorting her photographs into files on her computer, making them easier to find when needs be. Some had benefited from a little electronic enhancement and she was pleased with the results she'd achieved. She glanced at the kitchen clock, realising that it was well after lunchtime and wondering whether to bother making herself something to eat, when her phone, sitting on the table in front of her, buzzed with an incoming text message. The text was from a number neither she nor her phone recognised and it was urgently short:

MAGNOLIA WARBLER. ANCOMBE VALE.

Feldrake's heart skipped a beat. Messages like this appeared on her phone only very rarely, when other twitchers wanted to spread the news about a special sighting. The magnolia warbler was not a native UK bird. She was pretty sure it was an American species and reached for the bird book lying on the table next to her laptop. She was right. The magnolia warbler was a little bird that liked to travel. It spent the winter in the Caribbean and the summer in the United States or Canada. It did not, habitually, spend any time in Europe. This one, Feldrake reasoned, must have been a late traveller, heading north into the US but carried off course all the way to England by the storm that had swept across the Atlantic. There was no time to lose. Other twitchers

would already be on their way, including Stella Smart –
or would she be? Would she have received this message?
She wasn't widely admired in the birdwatching community after all, was she? Many saw her as overbearing,
domineering, even obnoxious. Would anyone have both-
ered contacting her? Maybe the magnolia warbler was
a trophy she could capture on camera without dear old
Stella ever even knowing about it!

Jumping to her feet, she rushed over to the fridge
and grabbed a plastic container pre-packed with a few
snacks and a small bottle of fruit juice. She always kept
the pack at the ready, refreshing its contents every week.
As a dedicated birdwatcher, she was constantly prepared to act the instant a rumour reached her about a
special sighting. The pack would keep her going while
she searched for the magnolia warbler. Carrying the
food pack and her camera bag, she grabbed a yellow
waterproof from a coat stand in the hall and hurried out
to her car. She smiled as she dropped into the driver's
seat and started the engine. Her little blue hatchback
might not be as grand as Stella's car, but it would get her
to Ancombe Vale before Miss High-and-Mighty Smart!
She turned left out of Tweeting Bottom, picturing the
perfect place to park in the Vale – a lay-by not far from
the river. From there she could walk into the woods
where the warbler was most likely to be found. She
sighed. The woods were on Guy Fawkes's land but no
matter, this was far too important to worry about that
awful man!

*

Following her disturbed night, Agatha slept late on Saturday morning, then gave in to the yowling of the cats and made her way downstairs to feed them. She was wearing a fluffy pink onesie, something she had bought on impulse some time ago and somehow never got round to throwing out, though she had to admit it was incredibly comfortable.

'Normally,' she said to herself, giving her reflection a stern look in the hall mirror, 'you wouldn't be seen dead dressed like this.'

She shrugged, headed for the kitchen and casually wondered what choice she would have in the matter. What would she be seen dead in? It was hardly likely she would have any kind of forewarning of her imminent demise. There probably wouldn't be time to change. If there were, she would choose something colourful but elegant and her make-up would be immaculate. She would be found in a dramatic yet serene pose, draped gracefully across the sofa in her living room. She shrugged. Who was she kidding? She'd seen plenty of corpses and none of them ever looked anything other than dead. True, some had been messier than others, but none were to be admired. There was no dignity in death. When life walks out on you, it takes all the good stuff with it.

Why was she being so morbid? She needed coffee. She fed the cats, then collected her newspaper and a sheaf of junk mail from the doormat before sitting down at the kitchen table for her first caffeine hit of the day. She was still sitting there over an hour later, working her way through one of the weekend supplements, when her phone rang. It was John. She smiled. She'd been looking forward to talking to him.

'I was wondering when you'd get round to calling,' she said. 'If the morning paper's anything to go by, I'm guessing you had a difficult drive home last night.'

'It took over four hours,' John said, and Agatha could hear him stifling a yawn. 'Normally I'd do that trip in half the time but there were all sorts of hold-ups – flooding and tree debris on the roads.'

'How are you feeling?' Agatha asked. 'That must have been so frustrating.'

'I'm a bit tired, but I'm okay. Listen, there are a few things we need to talk through. How about an early dinner at the Feathers in Ancombe? I can pick you up around six thirty.'

'Sounds good to me. What sort of things need talking through?'

'It's this Norwegian cruise . . .' he said, sounding decidedly unenthusiastic. 'I'm not sure about it all. I just need . . . Well, I need you to help me get things straight in my mind.'

'Well, I find there's nothing that straightens the mind better than a good dinner and a few glasses of wine.'

By the time she hung up, Agatha was already trying to decide what to wear. She wanted to look her best for dinner with John, yet didn't want to look overdressed. The Feathers was a traditional pub, all low ceiling beams and horse brasses, but it served very good food – several steps up the culinary ladder from Agatha's Carsely local, the Red Lion. It was also several steps up the pricing ladder from the Red Lion, which gave it a slightly pretentious character. People who could afford to eat there could also afford to dress well. She needed something that would look just right – not overly dressy, yet not too casual.

She ran through her wardrobe in her mind as she trotted upstairs, then rummaged through the hanging racks, holding one outfit after another up against her onesie while she studied them in a full-length mirror. She cast skirts, tops and dresses aside this way and that, ultimately convincing herself that she simply had nothing to wear. She needed to go shopping. A glance at the time on the radio alarm clock on her bedside cabinet told her she had barely five hours until John was due to pick her up. Not enough time for a trip to her favourite haunts in London's West End. There was, however, one reasonably upmarket department store on Mircester High Street where she had found some surprisingly decent outfits in the past. There was no time to lose. She hit the shower and prepared to do battle with Mircester's crowds of Saturday-afternoon shoppers.

'No! That's not good enough! Listen to me, you clown!' Stella Smart was bawling into her mobile phone loud enough to melt the mouthpiece. 'Shut up! Don't you dare try to talk over me! I told you to listen, didn't I? You listen with your ears, not your mouth, last time I checked! I don't care if you have to get your lazy, good-for-nothing lackey to work all through Sunday – I want those figures on Monday morning. Not Tuesday. Not Wednesday. Monday morning!'

She held the phone above the desk in her study as though to slam it down, then relented and tapped the icon to end the call. Who ever thought that was a good idea? A tiny little tap was no use at all. The best thing about the old phones was that you could slam the handpiece back into its cradle when you felt like it. It was therapeutic. It helped to get whatever moron you'd been talking to out of your head so you could get on with the rest of your day. Whoever you'd been talking to also knew that the phone had been slammed, so the slam had the extra benefit of letting them know you weren't to be trifled with. Maybe somebody should invent a slammable smart phone. She almost dropped the thing when it suddenly beeped and vibrated in her hand. A text message was displayed on the screen:

MAGNOLIA WARBLER. ANCOMBE VALE.

Smart read the message again. She knew the magnolia warbler was a very rare visitor to the Cotswolds – or anywhere else in the UK, for that matter. She guessed that a well-meaning twitcher had sent this message out to everyone on their contacts list, so important was the sighting. She simply had to add the warbler to her list of conquests. Grabbing her binoculars and car keys, she hurried to her front door, kicking off her shoes in the porch to pull on a pair of wellington boots – the kind that the Queen might wear at Sandringham or Balmoral. Her black barge of a car stood obediently in the driveway close to her front door. She threw a waxed field jacket inside and heaved herself in behind the wheel. Ancombe

Vale was only a few minutes away. With any luck, she'd be one of the first there.

Agatha Raisin was feeling very pleased with herself. In Mircester, she had found a midnight-blue 'georgette' dress with cap sleeves and a plunging neckline. It had a very flattering cut, the hem swirling gently at the knee, and was cinched at the waist with a silver-clasped belt. She had almost decided against buying the dress, feeling that it needed something to complete it as an outfit when, in a different department of the store, she spotted a bolero jacket of almost exactly the same dark blue, a swirling flower pattern woven into the fabric to give it some texture and a sprinkling of tiny silver sequins adding a touch of glamour. The jacket and dress were a match made in heaven and, sitting in the passenger seat of John's car, she would have felt divinely elegant had it not been for the fact that a small jazz devil was playing bongo drums in her stomach. She was ravenously hungry and it suddenly dawned on her that she hadn't actually eaten all day. The menu at the Feathers would offer all sorts of culinary delights, but at that moment she'd happily have wolfed down a plate of fries and a giant burger ... with cheese ... and extra fried onions ... and extra fries. That would not be on offer, but she knew the Feathers' menu so well that she could picture it in her mind and began choosing what she would order instead. That, of course, made her even more hungry.

Her preoccupation with food meant she was scarcely

following John's conversation, and both were taken by surprise when they rounded a bend on the narrow, hedge-lined country lane to be confronted with a queue of stationary cars and the ominous blue flashing lights of emergency vehicles.

There were only four cars in front of them but it seemed like more because of the police car and ambulance at the head of the queue. There were also three vehicles parked in the lay-by on the other side of the road. One was a large black car, one was a small blue hatchback and the other, the only one facing back the way they had just come, was a silver saloon. The immediate cause of the backed-up traffic was obvious – a large beech tree had fallen across the road, blocking it completely.

'What's going on here?' Agatha wondered, unclipping her seatbelt. 'Why the blue lights?'

'No idea,' John said, cutting the engine. 'Let's go take a look.'

They approached a small gathering of people, clearly the occupants of the other cars, who were being shep-herded by a uniformed police constable.

'Stay back, please,' the constable instructed the crowd. 'Let these people get on with their jobs.'

The paramedics from the ambulance could be seen on the far side of the tree along with another police officer and a number of people in civilian clothes. A slim man wearing a sports jacket and flannels stood in front of the tree, watching what was happening on the far side, his hands on his hips, his back to the crowd.

'What's happening, Kenny?' John called to the nearest uniformed policeman.

'There's been an accident and—' the officer began, then realised to whom he was talking. 'Oh . . . it's you, sir.'

'Not "sir" any more, Kenny,' John said, smiling. 'Just John. What's the story here?'

'Yes, what *is* the story?' John and Agatha were joined by a slightly built young woman with dark hair and spectacles that were fashionably too large for her elfin features. Agatha immediately recognised Charlotte Clark, a reporter with the *Mircester Telegraph*. She had been a trusted ally on many occasions in the past and Agatha had a healthy respect for her. 'According to my sources,' Charlotte went on, 'there's been a fatality.'

'I really can't say, miss,' the policeman said nervously.

'Give him a break, Charlotte,' Agatha said quietly. 'The constable can't tell you anything but I can see a man who can.' Agatha then called and waved to the man in the sports jacket. 'Bill! Over here!'

Bill Wong, a detective sergeant with Mircester Police and one of the first friends Agatha had made when she moved to Carsely, turned when he heard his name. Tall and handsome, Bill gave Agatha a gentle smile that failed to banish the grave expression on his face. He walked towards her, indicating a spot to the side of the small crowd where Agatha and John joined him, Charlotte hovering inquisitively in the background.

'We've got a really tragic situation on our hands here,' Bill said, keeping his voice low. 'A woman has been killed by the falling tree. I take it you're in one of the cars that's been held up?'

40

'We were on our way to the Feathers,' John said.

'So were we,' Bill said, nodding in the direction of a small group who had emerged from the woods, having walked round the base of the tree where giant roots were reaching skywards, clods of earth clinging desperately to them. Bill's wife, Detective Constable Alice Wong, was leading an older couple onto the road, accompanied by a female paramedic and a large woman wearing a waxed jacket. 'First night off we've had together in ages. Alice's parents are babysitting.'

'That's Miss Smart, isn't it?' Agatha said, recognising the imposing figure with the paramedic. 'And isn't that Miss Carstairs with Alice?'

'Obviously you know those ladies,' Bill said as the small group approached. 'I'm afraid they've had a terrible shock.'

Alice nodded a polite 'hello', leading Mary Carstairs and a man Agatha didn't recognise towards the silver saloon car. Stella Smart stopped when she spotted Agatha. She looked pale, her walk having lost its swagger and her appearance lacking its usual bluster.

'Mrs Raisin,' Smart said slowly, 'something terrible's happened. It's Joan . . . She's dead!'

'Dead?' Agatha said, taken by surprise. 'What on earth happened? How did . . .?'

She fell silent as she followed Smart's gaze towards the tree.

'Miss Feldrake was hit by the tree?' Agatha said, aghast. 'Oh, Miss Smart, I'm so terribly sorry.'

'We'd been friends for nearly sixty years,' Smart said.

'Look, if there's anything I can do,' Agatha said,

rummaging in her handbag for her card, 'please do give me a call.'

'Thank you, Mrs Raisin,' Smart said, tucking the card into a pocket. 'I will.' She then walked slowly past, heading for her car.

'A very nasty accident,' Bill said. 'Seems she'd been out in the woods and was heading back to her car when the tree fell on her. According to the paramedics, she didn't stand a chance. Massive head trauma.'

'The poor woman,' Agatha said. 'I can scarcely believe it. I was talking to her only yesterday evening!'

Agatha explained about the twitchers' talk at the church hall, without going into any of the details about Fawkes's intrusion.

'I'm sorry about your friend,' Bill said.

'She wasn't really a friend,' Agatha replied, 'but it's still a bit odd. I mean, what on earth was she doing wandering around in the woods on her own?'

'According to Miss Smart,' Bill said, 'she was probably out looking for a rare bird.'

'Were they all out birdwatching?' Agatha asked. 'Miss Carstairs doesn't look like she's dressed for it – and who's that man with her?'

'I can't go into it all right now, Agatha,' Bill said. 'I need to get a few more officers down here. We need to get these cars turned round, close the road further down and put diversions in place.'

'Is there anything I can do?' asked John.

'No, thank you,' Bill said, looking grateful for the offer. He seemed to appreciate talking to someone who understood his predicament. 'I've got other officers on their way, but we're incredibly stretched right now. There's flooding and trees down all over the county, so it looks like Alice and I will have to postpone our big night out. Miss Feldrake's friends are in no condition to drive, so I'll arrange for them to be taken home and then sort things out here. We'll have to cancel our dinner reservation.'

'I can at least do that for you,' John said, reaching for his phone. 'I'll have to let them know that we'll be a little late anyway. We'll have to go round by a longer route. That's if you still want to go, Agatha?'

'Why wouldn't I?' she responded, seeming distracted, staring at the cars in the lay-by and the fallen tree with a frown. 'I'm famished.'

The small crowd dispersed, ushered back to their cars to begin the tortuous, see-saw business of manoeuvring back and forth across the narrow lane in order to turn round and drive back the way they had all come. The fallen tree would remain blocking the road for quite some time. With no one to stop her, Agatha took the opportunity to venture a little closer to the tree and could see a couple of cars on the other side also being turned around by the police. She also caught a glimpse of Joan Feldrake lying under the tree, her yellow waterproof starkly bright and clean. She couldn't see the head wound and felt slightly ghoulish in craning her neck to try to look past the paramedic who was kneeling by the body, closing up his medical bag.

She looked at the tree's broken branches, its massive trunk and the web of roots, some quite spindly, some as thick as her arm, all torn violently from the ground.

'Sad, isn't it?' Charlotte Clark was shadowing Agatha. She had a notepad and pencil in her hands. 'A middle-aged woman's life has come to a tragic end, as has the life of a tree that could be around three hundred years old. This tree was probably here before both world wars, before Queen Victoria was born, before the USA existed . . .'

'I hope that's not how you're going to write up your report, Charlotte,' Agatha cautioned her. 'Your editors will want to see all the things that editors always want in stories like this. They'll want to know exactly how she died, exactly how old she was and they'll want you to mention money – how much she used to earn, how much her house is worth, if she was married, if there are any family members who will inherit – the usual thing. They won't want you crapping on about some crummy old tree.'

'I know, and I'll write it up just the way they want it,' Charlotte said, 'but the tree is so huge, such an enormous living thing . . . it just makes me think there must be more to this story.'

'You know, Charlotte,' Agatha said, staring once more at the tree roots, 'I think you may well be right. Look at those roots. They didn't leave the earth without putting up a struggle. They were ripped from the ground. Then there are all these broken branches . . .' She kicked at a shattered limb, turning things over in her mind, then looking up at the nearby treetops. 'The old tree clearly snapped off some really hefty branches as though they were just twigs when it came crashing down through the other trees.'

'It didn't give up without a fight, did it?' Charlotte said.

'No, it didn't,' Agatha agreed, 'and that fight would have been very noisy. It would also have happened relatively slowly. There's no way Miss Feldrake wouldn't have heard the tree roots being torn up or the whole thing gradually come crashing down. She would surely have noticed and . . .'

'And had time to get out of the way,' Charlotte said, tapping her pencil on the notebook. 'Maybe she wasn't much of a runner but she'd surely have seen the tree falling and been able to take just a few steps either up or down the lane here to keep herself safe.'

'It's possible she couldn't move,' Agatha pondered. 'I've seen people paralysed with fear . . . but this is a different situation. She wouldn't have been frightened in that sort of way. She would have been able to move out of the way.'

'Are you saying you think there's something fishy about all this?'

'What I'm saying is that I think it's all a bit weird.'

'If you start looking into it, will you keep me informed?' Charlotte asked.

'If you hear anything from your sources, will you do the same for me?' Agatha countered.

They looked each other in the eye, each giving the other a slight nod. A deal had been struck.

'Agatha, we need to get going,' John called, waving from the car, which he had turned to face back down the lane. 'We're just getting in the way here.'

'Enjoy your dinner, Mrs Raisin,' Charlotte said. 'Let's keep in touch.'

Chapter Three

The dining area at the Feathers was set aside from the main bar, the old building's layout working fortuitously to create a calmer, quieter ambience for diners than the more exuberant atmosphere enjoyed by the regulars at the bar. There was a certain harmony to the arrangement that helped to create the pub's unique charm. The hubbub of conversation from the bar wasn't too intrusive in the dining area, yet it made the whole place feel alive.

Agatha felt herself relax as soon as she walked in. They passed several other couples when the waiter showed them to their table and Agatha had a warm, smug feeling when she heard one woman hiss quietly to her husband, 'That's *exactly* the dress I want!'

Her conversation with John in the car had revolved mainly around the quickest route to the restaurant and the havoc that had been wreaked upon the countryside by the storm. John even had to guide the car carefully through a small pond in the road where the river had burst its banks. It was only two miles on the most direct route from Carsely to Ancombe, but the diversion made it ten. By the time they had settled in their chairs, Agatha had no doubt what to have when the waiter asked for their drinks order.

'Gin and tonic, please!' she said, and John ordered the same.

'You know,' he said, picking the cloth napkin off the table and smoothing it in his lap, 'that unfortunate business with the tree completely threw me off what I wanted to talk to you about.'

'It was all really strange, wasn't it?' Agatha replied, completely missing the way John was trying to steer the dialogue and focusing instead on the accident. 'You felt it, too, right? It just didn't seem possible that that poor woman was killed by a falling tree. It simply doesn't add up. I mean, now that I think about it, the ghastly yellow waterproof thing she was wearing hardly had a mark on it. That's not really what you'd expect when someone's been crushed by a tree, is it?'

'No, I suppose not, but—' John attempted to intercede.

'And another thing,' she continued. 'When I saw those women last night giving their birdwatching talk, Miss Feldrake looked pretty fit and able. Why didn't she manage to get out of the way of that tree in time?'

'Surely you're not seeing this as anything other than a tragic accident?'

'Of course I am!' Agatha's voice was now rising above the level of polite restaurant chat, approaching the volume of general debate in the bar. 'Last night I heard a man threaten to "exterminate" those three women and today one of them is dead!'

'Oh, for goodness' sake! You can't murder someone by clobbering them with a whole tree!' John was clearly exasperated, but quickly realised that he, too, was starting to raise his voice, attracting bemused looks from their fellow diners. He swallowed hard, staring into his lap, aware that Agatha was glowering at him across the table. He smoothed his napkin once more and chuckled. 'Look at us . . . bickering like . . .'

'An old married couple,' she said, and John looked up to see her expression had changed. She was smiling. No doubt it helped that their drinks were being served. Then Agatha Raisin did something that would have amazed anyone who knew her, and even surprised herself. She had a sip of her drink and gave ground.

'Let's not talk about the "accident" any more,' she said calmly. 'You wanted to discuss the Norwegian cruise.'

'I did,' he said, then hesitated, 'but maybe it's not . . .'

'It's important to you, so it's important to me, too,' she assured him.

'Well, they've offered me the job . . .'

'I never expected they wouldn't. You're too good.'

'. . . but it's not what I expected.' He took a deep breath and carried on. 'The ship sails in three weeks. It's a two-week cruise, but it's followed by a short break before another two-week cruise and that would be the pattern for the next six months. I would end up spending as much time away as I did at home.'

'I see,' Agatha said, staring straight in his eyes. 'Is that what you want?'

'No . . . I mean yes, but . . . I don't want to spend all that time away from you.'

'And I really miss you when you're away,' she admitted, 'but maybe that's something we just have to deal with.'

49

'It's not ideal for us to be apart for so long.'

'Perhaps it helps us appreciate what we have when we're together.'

'Perhaps . . . but I was thinking that . . . if you felt the same way . . . you could come with me. Maybe we could possibly think about getting—'

'If you were about to say "married",' Agatha interrupted, holding up a finger to stop him in his tracks, 'then hold it right there. We've both tried that, remember? You've been married before, and I've been married . . . a couple of times . . . and it didn't go too well for either of us, did it?'

She paused for a second, sipped her drink again, wagged the finger when he looked like he was about to speak, then carried on.

'We both have our own lives to lead and I want you to be part of my life, but that doesn't mean we have to be joined at the ship . . . I mean hip. What we have is special and I want to keep it that way. I don't want to ruin it by letting you think I want to stop you from doing what you so clearly enjoy. *Terrine de campagne* followed by lamb shank.'

The last was directed at the waiter, who had arrived with menus which he realised were unnecessary when John nodded that he'd have the same. The waiter scurried off.

'You think we can have the best of both worlds?' John asked.

'Why not?' Agatha said, smiling. 'We can have our cake *and* eat it. Actually, I'm rather fond of cake . . . maybe a bit too fond . . . Anyway, a very dear friend recently gave me some excellent advice. She told me that we should do our very best to enjoy our time together. I think that's what we should always aim to do.'

'Well, I'm all for that,' John said, raising his glass. 'Here's to us, and enjoying every moment together.'

'To us,' Agatha said, touching her glass against his. 'Now, what sort of wine shall we have with our dinner?'

'Your choice,' he said. 'I can't really drink any more. I'm driving.'

'You could always leave your car here,' Agatha suggested. 'We'll take a taxi back to my place and I can drive you over to pick up your car tomorrow.'

'I like that plan,' he said. 'Then we can enjoy every moment together all night.'

Late the following morning, Agatha drove John back to the Feathers. They had to take the diversion, the most direct route still blocked by the fallen tree, but that at least allowed them to enjoy more of the breathtaking Cotswold scenery. The wind had died down to a gentle breeze and, while the flooding and the debris on the roads still bore witness to the recent storm, the rolling hills and fields had shrugged off the weather's worst harassment to luxuriate in gentle sunshine.

A handful of other vehicles had been left in the Feathers' car park overnight, but there was no one around when Agatha and John stepped out of her car. He fished his keys out of his jacket pocket, pressed the button to unlock his car and dropped the keys back in his pocket. He then wrapped his arms around Agatha who, given that no one was watching, laughed as she submitted to the mighty bear hug, something she'd normally regard as an unacceptable display of public affection. He kissed her and smiled, easing his hold a little.

'I know you're back at work tomorrow,' he said, 'and I have chores to take care of today, then I'll be involved in preparing for the cruise, which is going to mean a lot of buzzing back and forth between here and Southampton, but we'll still make time for each other, won't we?'

'Of course,' she said. 'In any case, I may need to pick your brains.'

'What about?'

'Well . . .' she said slowly, 'will there be a police investigation into the death of Joan Feldrake?'

'You did really well,' he said, laughing and releasing her from his hug.

'What do you mean?'

'I wondered how long it would take you to bring up the accident again and you've managed to resist it for at least fifteen hours!'

'That's not fair!' she said, the shadow of a scowl crossing her face. 'I wanted us to have a nice time but I—'

'I know, I know,' he said, calming her. 'If you didn't want to get to the bottom of what happened to that poor woman, then you wouldn't be Agatha Raisin. You wouldn't be the woman I fell in love with.'

'So you'll help me look into it?'

'I'll do whatever I can. Bill Wong and his team will take statements from whoever found the body or was there at the scene – including us – then he'll submit a report, as will the pathologist. If it was me, I'd want to clear this one up quickly. It's all fairly straightforward and there doesn't appear to be any crime involved.'

'I'm not so sure about that, but . . .' Agatha noticed another car pulling into the car park. 'Looks like other people have arrived to pick up their cars. We'd best get out of the way. Call me later.'

With that, she jumped back in her car and headed home to Carsely.

There was no *Mircester Telegraph* on Sunday, but the 'Woman Killed by Falling Tree' story had made minor headlines on the inside pages of the nationals. Agatha had the papers spread out beside her on the sofa in her living room. She also had her iPad to hand, and when she viewed the *Mircester Telegraph*'s website she saw that the nationals were actually running a heavily edited version of the story written by Charlotte Clark, which appeared in full online. The website was updated even if there was no print edition on Sunday. Charlotte described Joan Feldrake as unmarried and living in a £350,000 house in Tweeting Bottom. She had even included a reference to the tree having been around since before the Battle of Trafalgar. Agatha smiled, wondering how hard Charlotte had had to negotiate to get that single historical reference past her editor. At that moment, her phone rang. It was none other than Charlotte Clark.

'Charlotte!' Agatha said. 'How funny – I was just enjoying your piece online. It reads well.'

'Thanks, Mrs Raisin,' Charlotte said, 'but I have to keep this brief. Rushing off to cover a car crash. What I wanted to say is that the man with Mary Carstairs was Anthony Feldrake, the dead woman's brother. I hear Anthony and Mary have recently become a couple.'

'Interesting,' Agatha said, intrigued. 'That's not a crime, of course, but it may add another dimension to the situation.'

'The old dears . . . I mean, neither Mary Carstairs nor Stella Smart will talk to me,' said Charlotte. 'If you dig up anything else on them . . .'

'I'll let you know, Charlotte,' Agatha assured her.

Agatha sat for a moment, pondering this new information. Did it really make any difference? Only time would tell. Hodge suddenly appeared, leaping up to land on the sofa in the middle of the *Sunday Times'* fashion pages. Agatha tutted at him and then Boswell came cantering into the room in hot pursuit of another bluebottle.

'I hope you're not going to make a habit of eating those,' she scolded him, before evacuating the living room for the peaceful sunshine in the garden. No sooner had she relaxed into a garden chair than her phone rang again.

'Agatha, darling!' came the voice of Roy Silver, a London friend Agatha had known for years. He had once worked for her when she ran her own PR agency and had been an invaluable asset when he'd helped out on past investigations. Roy still lived in the capital and still worked in the PR business, when he wasn't visiting the Cotswolds. 'I bet you're shut up indoors with the boring old Sunday papers, aren't you? How do you fancy a spot of absolutely gorgeous fresh air instead?'

'Actually, Roy, I'm enjoying the sunshine in my garden right now,' Agatha replied. 'I take it you're at Tamara's place.'

'Exactly,' Roy replied. 'I've been helping tidy up after that hellish storm and exercising the horses.' Roy had fallen in love with horse riding while working on a case with Agatha and had become a regular visitor to Tamara Montgomery's stables. 'The thing is, we're having a bit of a barbecue this afternoon about three-ish and wondered if you'd like to come along.'

'To tell you the truth,' Agatha said, even though she knew she was about to do precisely the opposite, 'I'm a bit busy this afternoon.'

'Oh, but you must come, darling,' gushed Roy. 'We're having one of Tamara's neighbours here, a lovely lady – Jessica Barnes – and she'd really like to meet you. She might need your professional help, you see. She's the victim of a sheep rustler!'

'Really, Roy, that's something to be dealt with during office hours and—'

'But you haven't heard the best bit yet, darling,' trilled Roy. 'The prime suspect has the most fabulous name – Guy Fawkes!'

'Three o'clock? I'll be there.'

Agatha took a leisurely shower, then washed her hair while mentally sparring with a dilemma she'd floored many times in the past, but which had the predictable and annoying habit of picking itself up to fight back again and again. It had nothing to do with work, nor anything to do with murder – it was far more serious than that. What was she going to wear?

Then she remembered an outfit she'd spotted during

the raid on her wardrobe the previous day and, her hair wrapped in a towel, she took a more leisurely look in the wardrobe, retrieving a pale cream waistcoat and shorts. She recalled the material having been described by the fashion house as 'crease-free natural linen'. It had better be. When she'd experimented with linen in the past, after about half an hour she'd looked like she was wearing a crumpled fish-and-chips wrapper. Having wandered through from the bathroom wearing nothing but the towel on her head, she stood in front of her mirror to try the linen ensemble against herself. The problem was immediately obvious. Her legs were way too pale. A little fake tan would soon sort that out. She'd apply it in moderation. She was going for healthy English rose rather than sun-baked beach babe, after all.

Attending to her hair and make-up always seemed to take more concentration and vigilance with the passing of time. Younger women like her office right-hand-person Toni, or the lovely Alice Wong, couldn't possibly appreciate how much of a blessing they enjoyed in having smooth, maintenance-free complexions. Still, youth wasn't everything. She wished she had known all the things she knew now when she was closer to their ages. The big advantage, however, of being ... more experienced ... was knowing how to make the most of your assets. She'd always thought her legs her best feature and a touch of colour would be perfect for them. Her face, however, needed her full attention. Using excruciatingly expensive creams, she massaged pesky wrinkles into oblivion and eradicated any stray hairs with deadly accurate tweezers. Despite the concentration demanded by her beauty regime, she couldn't stop her mind drifting to the mysterious Guy Fawkes. Clearly, he could be deeply unpleasant and didn't give a damn what anyone thought of him, yet somehow she found him strangely compelling. Maybe this afternoon she would find out a little more about the man.

The road between Blockley and Draycott, much like the road between Carsely and Ancombe, and so many of the area's minor roads, was lined with trees and hedgerows. Unlike the Ancombe road, however, the Draycott road had been cleared of storm debris. Here and there, in roadside ditches, Agatha spotted heavy branches that someone had dragged aside as well as jagged scars of white wood on the trees where limbs had been cruelly ripped away by the storm's ferocious winds. Today's blue skies and warm sunshine, on the other hand, made the storm seem like ancient history. Agatha had the car's air conditioning working full blast. She didn't want to arrive looking overheated and sweaty from the drive and neither did she want to open the window. The rush of air would leave her hair looking like she'd been bungee jumping into a tornado.

She turned off the road onto a track that led through a patchwork of fields towards the small cluster of buildings that housed the Montgomery Stables. She'd visited Tamara's place before and was pleased to see that little had changed. On one side of the track was a copse of oak trees which, Agatha was relieved to note, had survived the storm relatively unscathed. Opposite was a paddock, where the surface was a mixture of sand and what Agatha recalled to be recycled carpet fibres. This was where horses and their riders trained. She was amazed the area looked so flat and pristine.

An old farmhouse stood beyond the training area and beside it was a small barn alongside an enclosure boasting a selection of brightly painted show-jumping gates and walls. She could see some horses grazing in the sunshine on the far side of the show-jumping area. It was all relaxingly bucolic. She parked beside the farmhouse, stepping out of her car to receive an enthusiastic welcome from a black Labrador, a gyrating bundle of energy, its tail whirling like a propeller. Agatha had never considered herself a pet lover when she had been younger. She'd been far too busy working, desperately saving every penny in order to leave home when she was growing up, and then far too busy working, striving to make a name for herself in London, ever to have time for any kind of pet. That had all changed when she had first arrived in Carsely and Bill Wong had given her a stray tabby kitten called Hodge. Boswell, another stray tabby she at first mistook for Hodge, came along a little later. Now, even though she knew her devotion to her pets meant she was in danger of becoming the kind of person she'd heard described as a 'childless cat lady', she couldn't imagine not having Boswell and Hodge to come home to.

The dog now demanding her attention was a different matter. She would never have confessed to anyone that she was a little wary of dogs. That would be showing weakness and Agatha Raisin was anything but weak.

Dogs, nevertheless, had quite a lot of quite large teeth, and the one in front of her was showing her plenty of them. Yet she knew it was a smile rather than a snarl. She knew this black Labrador.

'Hello, Piper,' she said. 'You remember me, don't you? You lay under the kitchen table and slept with your big warm jowls on my toes last time I was here, didn't you?'

Piper leaned into her, pushing his neck against her leg, demanding to be patted.

'Okay, we're friends,' Agatha said, ruffling the fur behind his ears, 'but if you drool on my linen shorts or stick a muddy paw on them, I'll punch your lights out, agreed?'

He looked up at her adoringly with his big amber eyes, his mouth open, his tail still wagging.

'You know full well I don't mean that, don't you?'

Piper sniffed at her leg then looked up at her again, his mouth closed and his head tilted inquisitively to one side.

'Fake tan,' she whispered, stooping to pat him again. 'Keep it to yourself – it's our secret.'

'Agatha! How lovely to see you again!' Tamara Montgomery appeared at the corner of the house, grinning and striding forward to greet her guest. When Agatha had last seen her, she'd been wearing a big, baggy sweater, muddy jodhpurs and even muddier boots. Today she was dressed in a spotlessly white V-neck T-shirt, khaki shorts and sandals. Somewhere in her late thirties, she had the fresh, rosy glow of a woman who spends a healthy life outdoors. Agatha was impressed. The Tamara she had first come to know had been a dowdy creature very much in the doldrums, a far cry from the lean, fit, happy woman standing before her now.

'Tamara, you look fantastic!' Agatha complimented her.

'Thank you,' Tamara said, patting a few stray hairs into place. 'You look amazing, but then you always do. I have to try a bit harder.'

Agatha took the compliment with a smile, avoiding any potential competition around which of them put the most effort into their appearance. She suspected that was a contest she would win.

'I brought a little something,' she said, reaching into the car to produce a bottle of champagne. 'It should still be chilled.'

Tamara thanked her effusively, then led her round the farmhouse to a garden area dominated by a flat expanse of lawn and a large patio furnished with a few hay bales and a large, round table surrounded by chairs. The table, laid for four, sat in the shade of a green parasol. Tamara disappeared through a door into the kitchen to put the champagne on ice just as Roy Silver emerged with a tray of sausages for the barbecue.

'Agatha, darling!' He greeted her with a huge grin, which lost its edge when he realised she was staring at what he was wearing – pale cream shorts with a matching waistcoat. 'Oh, dear – one of us will simply have to change . . .'

Agatha narrowed her eyes and, despite the warm afternoon temperature, he felt the chill of her icy stare.

'. . . and that would be me,' he said. 'Take the sausages, darling. I'll be back in a trice.'

He disappeared indoors and Agatha deposited the sausages on a small table beside a large, black, barrel-type barbecue. Piper immediately sat by the table, fixing the tray with an unwavering stare. Agatha pointed a warning finger at him.

'Piper, you stay away from those sausages,' Tamara said, emerging from the kitchen with plates of lamb chops and chicken thighs. 'Agatha, have you met Jessica yet?'

A petite woman with a round face and short dark hair followed Tamara out of the kitchen. She was carrying a bottle of Chateau Barfield and a glass for Agatha, awkwardly juggling the two in order to free a hand to shake. She smiled briefly but failed to make eye contact. If Agatha were being considerate, not a virtue for which she was renowned, she'd have classed Jessica Barnes as 'shy', but first impressions and the weak handshake were already persuading her to lean more towards 'insipid'.

'Would you like to try a glass while we wait for Roy?' Tamara asked. 'It's from the Barfield Estate. I think it's actually very nice.'

'It is,' Agatha said, accepting the glass. 'Charles's vines aren't producing yet, but the winery's doing a very good job with English grapes from other growers.'

'You know about the Barfield wine?' Jessica asked, pouring a thin measure for Agatha, then studying the bottle's label as though desperately searching for something to talk about.

'Sir Charles Fraith and I are old friends,' Agatha explained. 'I organised the big launch event for Chateau Barfield, with a little help from Roy.'

'That was a day to remember!' Roy said, reappearing from the kitchen. He was now wearing a dazzling short-sleeved shirt patterned with exotic birds and tropical flowers. 'What do you think? Perfect for a barbecue, isn't it?'

He twirled and posed, making Tamara laugh.

'We were the perfect team for Sir Charles's do up at Barfield House,' he said. 'It was hard work, mind you.'

'He's been putting in a lot of hard work here, too, Agatha,' Tamara said. 'He's spent most of the weekend clearing leaves and debris from the training area and settling it all flat again.'

'Manual labour?' Agatha said, raising an eyebrow. 'What on earth's got into you, Roy?'

'It's the antidote to sitting behind a desk in London, darling,' Roy said, flexing his biceps. 'Working in the stables most weekends this summer and riding whenever I can has got me in better shape than I've ever been!'

They chatted as Tamara began searing sausages and chicken on the barbecue, Jessica listening intently to the others talk, as though casual conversation were something she had never before experienced. The Chateau Barfield eventually gave way to the champagne, but Agatha took care not to overindulge in the wine, determined that she would drive herself home after their meal and intrigued to learn all about Jessica's problems with Guy Fawkes. She refrained from quizzing Jessica about him until they were all seated at the table with a delicious selection of barbecued meats, vegetables and salads arranged in front of them. Then she could resist it no longer.

'Roy mentioned that you keep sheep, Jessica,' she ventured.

'I do,' Jessica replied meekly, 'but I try not to talk about that too much. Once I get started, you see, I tend to go on a bit and I think some people seem to find sheep a bit boring.'

'I suppose they must,' Agatha agreed. 'That's why we have the idea that counting sheep will help you fall asleep, isn't it?'

'Counting sheep is what keeps me awake,' Jessica said, with a quiet sigh.

'Why's that?' asked Agatha. 'Do you have a big flock?'

'Not at all,' Jessica replied. 'I only have a dozen.'

'But the number keeps changing,' Roy said, wiggling his eyebrows to suggest some dark intrigue. 'Sometimes there are fewer, then the number's back to a round dozen.'

'Does that happen a lot?' Agatha asked Jessica.

'It's been happening a lot more lately,' she answered, staring at her plate. Agatha noticed that Jessica had a piece of the deliciously barbecued chicken nestling among her salad and potatoes but none of the other meats. Having always regarded a barbecue as a chance to indulge in a 'mixed grill', Agatha had gladly accepted a piece of chicken, a sausage and a lamb chop.

'Is this one of yours?' she asked Jessica, prodding her lamb with her fork.

'Oh, no!' Jessica said, clearly aghast at the thought.

'Jessica's flock are show sheep, Agatha,' Tamara explained. 'They've won prizes at lots of county shows.'

'There are beauty contests for sheep?' Agatha glanced

at Roy, her look leaving him in no doubt that she wanted to know she wasn't being pranked.

'There really are, darling,' Roy assured her. 'Not quite beauty contests. More like sheepy Crufts.'

'So you have champion sheep?' Agatha asked Jessica.

'Yes, my girls have all done very well,' she replied, producing a mobile phone from a pocket to show Agatha some photos. 'They're all Bowmonts – that's the breed. Mabel does ever so well at every show she's in. Gloria has won best in breed three times. Jemima has—'

'Wait a minute . . .' Agatha interrupted. 'Your sheep all have names?'

'Of course,' Jessica confirmed. 'How else would I tell them apart?'

'How else indeed?' Agatha said, studying the white faces and large, sad eyes of the creatures staring out at her from the screen of the smart phone while Jessica scrolled through a stream of photos. To her they all looked exactly the same. She couldn't see how naming them would help identify them in any way whatsoever.

'Olivia and Delia get on really well with Poppy and Selena but Mabel is a bit of a loner. She can be quite naughty and . . .'

Agatha reached for her wine, beginning to regret her decision to drive home. She glanced across the table at Roy, who shifted uncomfortably under a glare that was quite obviously saying, *How did I ever let you talk me into this?* Then, as Jessica launched into a convoluted tale about the exasperating pranks of mischievous Mabel, Roy finally piped up to redirect her.

'Why don't you tell Agatha about the disappearances,

Jessica?' he suggested. 'I'm sure she might be able to help.'

Agatha saw Jessica take a deep breath and decided she needed sustenance to see her through the sheep lady's next outpouring. She looked to her plate and was about to cut into a boiled potato when its shape and yellowy whiteness reminded her of the sheep photos she'd just seen – Poppy, or possibly Selena. She took a piece of chicken instead and pushed her lamb chop to the side of the plate. It seemed almost cruel to tuck into the tempting lamb with Jessica watching.

'Well, my bedroom window looks out over the little field where my girls live,' Jessica said, 'and I like to say goodnight to them all at bedtime. Recently, though, I've looked out and only been able to count ten, sometimes as few as nine of them, instead of twelve.'

'That must be really annoying when you're all ready for bed,' Agatha said, trying to sound sympathetic.

'Yes, very upsetting,' Jessica said quickly, apparently glad that Agatha understood. 'Three times I've gone out in the dark with a torch searching for the missing ones but found no sign of them. I've sat downstairs worrying until dawn and then, when I go out in the morning light, all twelve of them are there!'

'Maybe it's naughty Mabel and a couple of her chums playing tricks on you,' Agatha offered.

'No, it's definitely not that,' Jessica said, completely failing to hear the sarcasm in Agatha's remark. 'They've been taken during the night and then returned very early in the morning. Really quite sinister, don't you think?'

'I think it looks like you're not actually losing your

sheep,' Agatha said, then sipped her wine. 'Your marbles, on the other hand . . .'

Jessica gave Agatha a confused stare and there was a brief moment of uneasy silence hastily broken by Roy with the most unconvincing stage laugh Agatha had ever heard.

'Oh, ha-ha-ha!' he blurted. 'I told you you'd like Agatha, Jessica. She's such a joker, isn't she? Tell her about your neighbour, my dear. He was what really caught Agatha's interest when I called her.'

'Yes . . . of course,' Jessica said uncertainly. 'Fawkes – I think he's the one behind this. I think he's kidnapping the girls at night, then returning them before he thinks I'll notice.'

'Why would he do that?' Agatha asked.

'I don't know,' Jessica said, growing agitated. 'Maybe he's trying to drive me mad – or trying to drive me away from here. I've also heard that he carries out hideous experiments in the barn on his farm.'

'Experiments?' Agatha was intrigued. This was the second time she'd heard someone talk about Fawkes conducting experiments on his farm. On the basis that there was no smoke without fire, her suspicions were now aroused. 'What sort of experiments would he do on your animals?'

'I've really no idea,' Jessica said. 'I shudder to think.'

'Do you have any proof that he's been taking your sheep?' Agatha asked.

'I've seen him,' Jessica said, her voice dropping almost to a whisper. 'Not taking them, but I saw him carrying Delia – or was it Dolores? – over to the fence to put her

66

back in my field. A few minutes later, I saw him do the same with Jemima. Yes, definitely Jemima. None of the others has a smile quite like hers.'

'Were any of them injured in any way?'

'Not at all,' Jessica said, sounding relieved. 'In fact, he leaned over the wall to put them back in my field quite gently.'

'He was carrying a sheep and stretched across to place it "gently"?' Agatha said, holding out her arms as though weighing an invisible sheep. 'How much does one of your sheep weigh?'

'A little over forty kilos,' said Jessica.

'Which is . . .?' Agatha looked to Roy and Tamara, unsure of her metric measurements.

'Over ninety pounds,' Tamara said.

'That's a lot to be holding out, leaning over a wall,' Agatha said, letting her arms drop. 'He's quite a strong bloke.'

'But what was he doing with the sheep?' Roy sat back in his chair, cradling his glass of wine, satisfied that Agatha was now taking a genuine interest in Jessica's story.

'That, of course, is what we need to find out,' Agatha said. 'Have you talked to the police about this, Jessica?'

'I called them,' she said, nodding, 'and two nice young constables came round to see me. They told me there wasn't anything they could do because no animals had been harmed and there was no proof that they had been taken. They said that no crime had been committed, so there was nothing for them to investigate.'

'They didn't think there was anything suspicious

going on?' Agatha was appalled, but not really surprised. Mircester Police were notoriously understaffed and overworked.

'No, they said that a chief inspector had told them not to waste time on cases or complaints where it looked like they wouldn't get what they called "a good result",' Jessica replied.

'I think that will be our old friend DCI Wilkes, Agatha,' Roy said, beaming. He knew full well that the mere mention of Wilkes's name would be the final morsel of bait needed to lure her into the mystery.

'I think you might be right,' Agatha agreed, a slight scowl crossing her face when she looked at Roy across the table, but a calmer expression prevailed when she turned back to Jessica. 'Let me look into Mr Fawkes, Jessica. In the meantime, you should stay well away from him – don't say a word to him – but let me know straight away if there are any more incidents. We'll soon find out what's going on and keep your animals safe.'

'Thank you, Agatha,' Jessica said, heaving a great sigh of relief. 'My Bowmont girls mean the world to me.'

'Of course they do,' Agatha said, her attitude towards Jessica now transformed into gentle empathy. The conversation, however, needed a change of direction. 'Is the riding school as busy as ever, Tamara?'

They chatted over the remains of the meal and some excellent coffee before Agatha eventually decided it was time to leave. Roy walked her to her car.

'So what do you think of Jessica's problem with Fawkes?' he asked.

'Business a bit dull in London, Roy?' she replied,

rounding on him. 'It's the silly season, isn't it? Lots of people off on holiday and everything slowing down, so you came up here for a bit of fun and thought you saw the opportunity to get involved in something more exciting.'

'What? I mean—'

'Don't bother trying to deny it, Roy. We've known each other too long for that. You decided to get me involved with Jessica Barnes's little problem to spice things up around here.'

'I'm sorry,' he said. 'I didn't mean to upset you.'

'Apology accepted,' she replied. 'Consider yourself forgiven, but don't think I'm not aware of what you were doing. I don't like being played, Roy, so don't ever try to do that again. Don't worry, we're still friends, and I want you to stick around for a while. I may need you. Whatever is happening with poor Jessica's sheep may be just the tip of the iceberg here. There's something odd going on and I intend to get to the bottom of it. Guy Fawkes just became what investigators like to call a "person of interest".'

'I'll be here, Agatha. You can count on me.'

'Good, because all my instincts are telling me things are about to get serious.'

'How serious?'

'As serious as it gets, Roy – as serious as murder.'

Chapter Four

By the time Agatha arrived home, the soft light of the early-evening sun had blessed the buildings lining Carsely High Street with a tender glow, their Cotswold stone turning the colour of warm honey. The ancient limestone was what gave the buildings, and the entire area, its unique character. Just as she had been, home buyers were drawn to the welcoming cosiness of houses built using the local stone. A cottage like hers, with a thatched roof, was the postcard-perfect, romantic idyll, yet the stone wasn't just the stuff of small villages. Blenheim Palace and St Paul's Cathedral were built using Cotswold stone. James had taught her that.

Her former husband and current next-door neighbour, James Lacey was an ex-army officer turned military historian and travel writer. Agatha had fallen madly in love with this tall, straight-backed, handsome man when he had first moved to Carsely and had pursued him remorselessly, turning into something of a stalker when she even tracked him to foreign climes. At first, despite her best attempts to charm him, he hadn't seemed remotely interested. To her, that had presented a challenge verging on obsession, making James even more desirable.

She smiled when she remembered the tortuous beauty regimes and desperate dieting she had undertaken to try to make herself irresistible to him. Then she frowned a little. These days, now that she thought about it, she devoted just as much time to looking her best. Was she still putting so much effort into her appearance for John? She was reminded of the phrase, 'You don't keep running once you've caught the bus.' Well, she'd caught John, so why was she still running? Checking her mirror before signalling to turn into Lilac Lane, she looked herself briefly in the eye and sighed.

'It's you, isn't it?' she said to herself. 'I do it all for myself, don't I?'

The truth was, she liked to look good for herself, no one else. Other people were superfluous when it came to her appearance. Agatha Raisin always simply liked to look her best.

'And you can't catch a bus if you're driving it,' she said, smiling as she parked her car by her garden gate.

At this time of day, the sunshine was mainly on the front of her house, and, walking up the garden path, she heard James calling her.

'Agatha, my dear! Can I have a word? Come and join me!'

He was sitting in the sunshine by his front door, a small table to his right, beside which was a second chair. On the table stood a bottle of red wine and an empty glass. The glass in his hand was fully charged and raised in her direction. He was neatly dressed, as always, in a short-sleeved checked shirt and pale chinos with a knife-edge crease.

'That would be lovely,' she said. 'I'm not driving any-where else today, after all.'

She stepped over the low fence between their gardens, a manoeuvre she'd have been wary of performing had she been wearing a skirt or dress rather than her shorts, and took a seat as he filled her glass.

'Looks like you were waiting for me,' she said, and they clinked glasses.

'Well, I could see you were out and hoped to catch you coming home,' he said. 'The thing is, I'm going to be away for two or three weeks.'

'It's not . . .?' Her free hand drifted up unintentionally to touch the back of her head. James had a tumour that was inoperable. The last time he'd disappeared it was because he'd been rushed into hospital.

'Oh, no, nothing to do with that,' he said, dismissing the idea with a wave of his hand. 'The drugs the medics gave me are keeping that at bay. Actually, I'm doing a spot of work. My publisher wants me to take a trip to Iceland.'

'Are you feeling up to it?'

'Never better, my dear. Well, obviously I have been better, but I'm fighting fit and raring to go. Sitting around here's not doing me any good. I need to get back to the front line. Why don't you take a break and come with me?'

'It's sweet of you to ask,' she said, reaching out to touch his hand, 'but I can't really do that.'

'Ah, yes,' he said. 'I suppose people might think—'

'I don't really give a stuff about what people might think,' she said. 'John is going away, too. He wanted me to go with him as well. Seems the men I care most about want to whisk me off into the sunset.'

'Sun doesn't really set in Iceland at this time of year . . .'

'It was a figure of speech, James,' Agatha said with a little laugh. 'The thing is, I don't want to risk upsetting John by turning him down and then immediately jetting off with you. I wouldn't want him to feel . . . betrayed.'

'Yes, I can see that,' James said. 'You care about him a great deal, don't you?'

'Well, yes, but . . . that's not entirely the point,' Agatha said, suddenly feeling uncomfortable discussing her feelings for her lover with her ex-husband. 'I need to have my own life, and that life is here.'

'Everybody needs a holiday for a bit of rest and recuperation,' said James.

'I know that, but I'm the one who decides when I need a break and where I want to go,' Agatha said, then took a sip of wine.

The truth was, ever since she had decided to make her home in Carsely, leaving the village for any extended period made her feel slightly anxious. She knew that, no matter how hard she tried, she might never be accepted as a 'local'. She desperately wanted to belong, but she knew in her heart that only those born and bred in the Cotswolds could ever be considered anything more than an interloper. Anyone else, no matter how many years they lived there, no matter how hard they tried to integrate into the community, would always be outsiders.

Agatha would never admit to caring what people thought of her – as far as she was concerned, anyone who didn't like her could get knotted – but she wanted to *feel* like this was home. She'd left Birmingham for London and she'd left London for Carsely, knowing that this was where she wanted to be. If fitting in meant leaving as infrequently as possible, then that's what she'd do. If it meant listening to all the most scurrilous gossip to find out everything that was going on in the area, then she'd do that, too. Actually, the listening bit was more of a pleasure than a chore. She enjoyed finding out about people – that was what made her a good detective – and there was someone she needed to find out about now.

'Anyway, I'm busy at work,' she continued, returning her glass to the table. 'There's someone who's just become of professional interest and I need to know more about him.'

'Really, who is it?'

'Around here they call him Guy Fawkes.'

'Well, I know a good deal about him,' James said, looking surprised. 'He was a professional soldier. He was known as Guido when he fought alongside the Spanish in Europe in the fifteen nineties.'

'Actually, that's not the Guy Fawkes I'm— Wait a minute. He was Spanish?'

'No, he was from Yorkshire. The European war was more of a religious thing for him,' James explained. 'He was Catholic and fought for the Catholic King Philip of Spain against the Protestant Dutch Republic. When he came back to England, the Gunpowder Plot was also all about religion and regime change.'

'Well, I don't think I need concern myself about something that happened more than four hundred years ago.'

74

'Maybe not,' said James, 'but Fawkes knew what he was doing. He'd experimented with gunpowder during the war and packed enough under the old House of Lords to blow it to smithereens. He'd have killed everyone inside, including the king.'

'Experimented?' Agatha said. 'I keep hearing about experiments when people talk about my modern-day Fawkes. He seems to be a man everyone knows something about, but nobody really actually knows.'

'You need to be careful,' James advised. 'Things can turn nasty when you tangle with the wrong people.'

'I can look after myself, you know that,' Agatha assured him. 'Now, tell me all about your plans for Iceland . . .'

Agatha prided herself on getting to her office early. Not at the crack of dawn when early shift workers and farmers were starting their day, but early enough to bag her favourite spot in the municipal car park and be at her desk in good time to browse the newspapers before the real working day started. That, of course, was way before anything other than the coffee shops and snack bars were open in Mircester city centre. Some may have regarded that as a boon because it prevented them making any rash impulse purchases of things spotted in shop windows. It wasn't a problem Agatha struggled with. There was seldom anything in any Mircester shop window by which she felt even a teensy bit tempted and never any temptations that she couldn't resist.

One thing she could never resist, however, was checking herself out in the shop windows. She was especially pleased with the vibrant yellow dress she had picked up on a recent trip to London. It was light enough to wear on a warm summer day, but its modest V-neck and short sleeves made it suitable for business. The bodice held the shape reasonably tight to the waist from where the skirt flared to just below the knee. It was a retro style that she thought wouldn't have looked out of place on Grace Kelly or Audrey Hepburn. Skipping across the treacherous cobbles on the old lane leading to her office, she waved cheerfully to Mr Tinkler, who owned the antiques shop below Raisin Investigations, and wondered who she looked most like that day – Kelly or Hepburn? Neither. She wasn't like anyone else. She was Agatha Raisin. She opened the street door and trotted up the stairs to the office.

When she walked into the main, open-plan office area, she wasn't in the least surprised to see that her staff were all there already. She liked them to be punctual but knew they all made sure they were there when she arrived in order not to miss out on being part of any tasty new cases she might have up her short yellow sleeve.

'Hi, boss!' Simon Black, sitting on the edge of his desk with a cup of coffee in his hand, gave Agatha one of his trademark grins. His thin features wrinkled and the grin forced his pointed nose down towards his bony chin. Agatha had always thought him a strange-looking young man, although he never seemed to be short of female companions, and he had proved himself to be a brave, loyal member of the team. Today, however, he looked distinctly like he was letting the side down. His hair was greasy and unwashed, he hadn't shaved and he was wearing an ancient, faded 'Ramones' T-shirt over torn, grubby jeans. She lowered her head slightly, taking care not to create even the hint of a double chin, and stared at him from beneath her brows. His grin never wavered. He held his arms out as though presenting his outfit.

'I'm on surveillance in the shopping mall as soon as it opens, remember?' he explained. 'The shoplifters know all the store detectives, so I'm hanging out there today. Dress to fit in, you always say, and this is practically a uniform for the tossers who hang around there all day.'

Agatha raised her chin. 'Good thinking, Simon, but I don't like that word you just used and,' she paused and sniffed the air, 'despite the fact you haven't shaved, you've overdone the Hugo Boss cologne. Wash it off before you go out or the tossers will be on to you.'

Simon, still grinning, held up his hands in defeat and Toni Gilmour laughed at his over-dramatised act of surrender. Agatha used to think that Toni looked most beautiful when she remained cool and reserved. That had suited the ice-maiden image projected by her pale skin, blonde hair and startlingly blue eyes. Having left her teenage years behind and advanced into her early twenties, she had filled her frame just as her character had begun to define her features. When they were seen together in the past, Agatha had bristled when some took her to be Toni's mother. How could anyone think she was old enough to have a grown-up daughter? Now, even if Agatha thought her still a bit on the skinny side,

Toni looked so stunning that she accepted the mistake as a compliment.

'Morning, Agatha.' Toni smiled. 'Love that dress. Wish I could get away with that style.'

'Never mind,' Agatha consoled her. 'Maybe one day you'll have the figure for it.'

Patrick Mulligan grunted a greeting from behind his computer screen. A retired policeman, Patrick had the craggy, lined features of a man who, whatever he was doing, always looked like he'd far rather be sitting behind a pint in a quiet corner of a pub. Yet looks can be deceiving and Patrick's contacts, along with his years of experience, made him an invaluable investigator. Agatha gave what she hoped was a ladylike grunt in return, while heading for her own, private office.

Just as she did every morning, she dropped her handbag into one of the many drawers in her enormous desk, then looked up to see Helen Freedman, her secretary and the office admin angel, proffering her a cup of coffee, a document folder with pages marked for her attention and that morning's edition of the *Mircester Telegraph*. Undoubtedly the most organised person Agatha had ever met, Mrs Freedman was middle-aged, grey-haired, a tower of strength and an absolute treasure. Agatha thanked her, then circumnavigated her desk again to stand in her office doorway.

'Simon has to be out of here shortly,' she announced, 'so let's have a case conference in my office straight away.'

Her three detectives grabbed whatever they needed – phones, notebooks and relevant papers – then began the

Monday-morning ritual of dragging their chairs towards Agatha's office in their customary order. Toni was followed by Patrick, who was followed by Simon, while Mrs Freedman sat resolutely in the outer office, manning the phone and guarding the door like a terrier in Marks & Spencer gingham.

'Right,' Agatha said, watching everyone settle in and consulting her own notepad. 'Let's hear the latest, Toni.'

As Agatha's second-in-command, Toni kept up to date with all of the firm's current cases.

'Simon's starting the shopping mall surveillance today, as you know,' she began. 'I have the Alcock and Bracegirdle divorce cases. I've got some good evidence – including photos – of Mr Alcock cheating on his wife, but the Bracegirdle case is moving more slowly. Mrs Bracegirdle is very good at covering her tracks and . . .'

There followed a brief discussion about the divorce cases, the evidence Patrick was gathering for civil cases being handled by two firms of local solicitors and a handful of employee background checks the team was running between them for some corporate clients.

'I have some potential new business,' Agatha announced. 'Jessica Barnes believes her sheep are being taken by a man named Fawkes.' Agatha refrained from calling him Guy Fawkes in order to avoid any timewasting jokes that would inevitably come from Simon.

'Well, best not let him pull the wool over our eyes,' Simon said, and made the little finger-snapping, hand-clapping gesture that always annoyed Agatha. Toni and Patrick groaned at the joke. Agatha glowered at Simon.

'Isn't it time you were going?' she said, and he got up to leave, dragging his chair behind him, still chuckling at his own gag. 'And don't forget to wash!' Agatha called after him.

'So who is Fawkes?' Patrick asked.

'I think I'd like to look into him myself,' Agatha said, 'but I need the usual background information on Jessica Barnes as well as four others: Stella Smart, Mary Carstairs, Joan Feldrake and her brother Anthony Feldrake.'

'Joan Feldrake?' Toni said, frowning. 'Isn't she the woman who was killed in that horrible accident on Saturday?'

'The very same,' Agatha said, and went on to describe what had happened at the Ladies Society meeting when Fawkes threatened the twitchers. 'It could be that nothing comes of this, but there's something that doesn't feel right about Miss Feldrake's death. We need to be discreet. Find out everything you can about the Feldrakes and the others, but don't let any of them know we're snooping around, otherwise they might try to throw us off the scent.'

'Making threats like Fawkes did can actually be classed as common assault,' Patrick pointed out. 'He could be nicked if anyone reports him.'

'Let's hope no one does,' Agatha said. 'We can find out more about Mr Fawkes if he's not put on his guard by being arrested.'

'Where do we start?' Toni asked.

'Fawkes's farm is on the Barfield Estate,' Agatha said, 'so we can start by finding out what Sir Charles Fraith knows about him. I'll set up a meeting. I'd like you with me for that, Toni.'

Agatha was well able to handle Sir Charles on her own, but taking Toni with her would make any meeting more formal and perhaps avoid any efforts by Charles to rekindle their romantic relationship. His attempts to win her back had become tedious and she could do without all the verbal jousting required to fend off his advances. Losing her temper with him and giving him a roasting was always an option, but she wanted to remain friends and that wasn't the way to do it.

Toni and Patrick had just left her office when Mrs Freedman tapped politely on her door.

'There's a Mr Randall here to see you,' she said. 'He doesn't have an appointment.'

'Martin?' Agatha looked pleasantly surprised. 'Give me precisely one minute, then send him in.'

Agatha reached down to her handbag drawer, quickly locating a small compact and her lipstick. She made lightning-fast repairs, touching up the lipstick that had been disturbed by her coffee cup, snapping the compact mirror shut when she was happy with her efforts. Martin Randall might never be more to her than a business associate, but a girl still had to look her best when a gentleman came calling.

Randall dabbled in antiques and ran a successful auction house where Agatha had once bought an old clock that had subsequently plunged her into the heart of a murder. He had also been involved in a charity auction at Barfield House as part of the launch celebrations for Chateau Barfield.

'Agatha, how lovely to see you again!' Randall was tall with dark hair and had an elegant, relaxed charm. He wore an expensive shirt without a tie, a beautifully tailored suit and the kind of tan which, unlike Agatha's, clearly hadn't come out of a bottle. Agatha rounded her desk again to allow him a peck on the cheek in greeting.

'What brings you into town?' she asked, sitting back down behind her desk after offering him the only other chair in the small room.

'I am allowed out of that barn we call an auction house now and again,' he said, laughing, 'but I'm actually on my way to give some valuations for a few bits and pieces prior to a house being completely cleared. Apparently, there's some vintage camera equipment that could do well at auction. It's not the sort of thing I normally get involved in, but I thought you might be interested.'

'Why's that?'

'A friend of mine was caught in a bit of a traffic jam on Saturday and he said he thought he saw you there, too.'

'If he was in one of the cars held up by the fallen tree, then he did see me there.'

'He said you were having a word with the friends of the woman who was killed, Joan Feldrake.'

'He's right again. I had met Miss Feldrake only the previous evening.'

'The thing is . . .' Randall shifted in his chair as though something was making him feel uncomfortable. 'The house that's being cleared is Joan Feldrake's. Her brother has asked me to go along to Tweeting Bottom and take a look.'

82

'That seems disrespectfully premature,' Agatha said, appalled. 'I mean, the poor woman hasn't even been laid to rest yet!'

'I agree. It seemed very strange to me.'

'There are a lot of strange things surrounding the death of Joan Feldrake,' Agatha said.

'I knew you'd be thinking that,' said Randall, sitting back in his chair, almost as if congratulating himself on being right. 'I was going to turn down Mr Feldrake, but then I selfishly thought it might give me a chance to see you again. Would you like to come with me?'

'To a house clearance? You really know how to show a girl a good time, don't you?' Agatha said.

'Put it this way,' Randall said, with a persuasive smile. 'You think there was something strange about Joan Feldrake's death. I'm offering you the chance to take a look inside the dead woman's home, just as she left it.'

'That's an irresistible sales pitch,' Agatha said, opening her handbag drawer again. 'Let's go.'

Agatha had never before been to Tweeting Bottom but, as Randall guided his Mercedes around the small field in the middle of the development, she knew they were being observed.

'You know that creepy feeling you get when you're being watched?' she said, peering out at the front windows of one of the bungalows.

'I know what you mean,' he said, laughing. 'It's that sort of place, isn't it?'

'A nightmare for covert surveillance,' she said. 'You

can't be secretly watching someone when everyone round about is secretly watching you. It's a great burglar deterrent, though.'

'What is?'

'Nosy neighbours. They're the best home security you can ever have.' She spotted a driveway up ahead where two cars were squeezed in together – a blue hatchback and a silver saloon. She immediately recognised them as the ones she had last seen parked nose-to-nose in the lay-by beside the fallen tree. She pointed to the cars. 'I think it must be that house.'

Randall parked on the road, and no sooner had they stepped out of the car than the bungalow's front door opened. Anthony Feldrake and Mary Carstairs were waiting in the doorway. Following a brief round of introductions, Randall explained Agatha's presence by saying that they were on their way to a business appointment together. Agatha was impressed by how smoothly the lie had flowed. Had she been on the receiving end, even she might have swallowed it. Feldrake led them into the front room, a comfortably furnished living room, where a tray sat on a low table loaded with a teapot, cups, saucers, milk, sugar and a plate of chocolate digestives. The walls were hung with framed photographs of birds.

'All Joan's work,' Feldrake said, noticing Agatha perusing the photos. 'She had a good eye.'

'She certainly did,' Agatha agreed. 'I'm so sorry for you about what happened. It's a terrible tragedy. It must all have come as a dreadful shock.'

'I can hardly believe it,' he replied, inviting Agatha and Randall to take a seat on the sofa. 'Sitting here before you arrived, I kept looking up, expecting her to come in from the kitchen with more milk, or teaspoons or something.'

Miss Carstairs poured tea for them all.

'Shall we take ours through to the back room, Mr Randall?' Feldrake said, picking up his cup and saucer. 'That's where all Joan's camera stuff is, along with the antique bits and pieces.'

The two men left the room and there was a brief moment of silence while Agatha and Miss Carstairs sipped their tea.

'I'm sure this has all come as a huge blow to you as well, Miss Carstairs,' Agatha said, gently settling her cup back on its saucer. 'I understand you, Miss Smart and Miss Feldrake had been friends since you were at school.'

'We were,' Miss Carstairs confirmed, reaching into her handbag to retrieve a tissue and dab a tear from the corner of her eye. 'I haven't been able to sleep a wink since Saturday, Mrs Raisin. Every time I close my eyes, I see poor Joan lying there under that tree.'

She wiped away another tear, then opened the tissue and blew her nose.

'I think it's very brave of you to start dealing with the formalities so soon,' Agatha said. 'The house and its contents, I mean, when everything's still so fresh in your mind.'

'That was Anthony's idea,' Miss Carstairs said, composing herself. 'He's recently retired. He was an engineer. He's used to being active, always busy. He simply had to start looking into what should be done with the house

85

and all Joan's things. He said sitting doing nothing at a time like this would drive him mad.'

'I can understand that,' Agatha said. 'Sometimes you need to keep your mind occupied. I'll never forget the sight of that tree across the road. How did you come to be at the scene of the accident? Had you gone there with Miss Feldrake?'

'No, we were at the Feathers in Ancombe for afternoon tea,' Miss Carstairs explained. 'We called Joan to ask her to join us but she said she was out looking for a magnolia warbler and that she'd come along as soon as she could. She didn't really approve, you see.'

'Approve? Approve of what?'

'Of Anthony and me, Mrs Raisin,' Miss Carstairs said, holding her chin up in a defiant posture. 'Anthony's been living and working up north for years. His wife died last year and when he retired, he decided to come home. All of us were born and brought up around Carsely. Anthony and I used to be sweet on each other when we were young and, when he came home a few weeks ago, we got back together. Joan wasn't happy about it but we were determined to win her round. That's what the meeting at the Feathers was all about. We wanted her to see that we were happy and we wanted her to be happy for us. That was far more important to me than a spurious warbler sighting.'

'What a coincidence,' Agatha said. 'We were on our way to the Feathers when we got caught up in the accident.'

'It was all simply awful, wasn't it? We drove down there when Joan didn't show up and wasn't answering her phone. Anthony said he had a bad feeling and was worried something might have happened to her. Little did we know . . .'

'But you knew where she was?'

'Oh, yes. Joan, Stella and I have used that lay-by a lot when we've gone looking for birds in the woods and down by the river. We got there in no time and found her . . .'

Miss Carstairs sniffed, found a fresh tissue, dabbed her eyes and blew her nose again. Agatha stood and strolled to the window. A couple more framed photographs were perched on the window ledge along with two bird ornaments: a kingfisher and a heron. Agatha studied the ornaments and how they were positioned on the ledge. She then looked around the room at the sideboard, chairs and sofa and, even though she was standing in the sunshine streaming through the window, she felt a little shiver run down her spine. Something wasn't quite right in the room.

'Everything's very neat here,' she said, turning to look out of the window. 'The gardens are all very tidy and the houses look meticulous – no peeling paint or overflow-ing bins.'

'That's what Joan liked about this place,' Miss Carstairs said. 'She was a very neat person. She didn't get on with all of her neighbours, but she loved living here.'

'I'm sure she did,' Agatha said. 'That meadow out there seems a little out of character for the development, though. It all looks a bit wild and overgrown.'

'Ah, but it's a very special place,' Miss Carstairs said, managing a weak smile. 'When these houses were being planned, the developers were told to stay well clear of that little meadow because skylarks were known to nest there. They build their nests on the ground, you see. They're quite rare birds, but they still nest here and, of course, the male is famous for the song he sings when he soars high in the air. That's why the place is called Tweeting Bottom.'

'What a sweet story,' Agatha said, 'but what did you mean when you said she didn't get on with all her neighbours?'

'Oh, just a few gripes,' Miss Carstairs said with a shrug. 'Let's go and see how they're getting on in the other room.'

The two men were examining various items of photographic equipment when Agatha and Miss Carstairs walked in.

'Almost finished here,' Randall said, using his phone to photograph an old camera where the front opened and the lens extended on a bellows arrangement. It looked far too fragile and clumsy for Agatha's liking. She didn't like having to fiddle with bits of a camera to make things happen. In her line of work, she needed to be able to point and shoot, fast and accurate. She looked out of the window to the back garden, where something looking a little like a children's playhouse stood on stilts at the far end of the lawn. It was draped with camouflage tarpaulins.

'What's that at the bottom of the garden?' she asked Miss Carstairs.

'That's the hide Joan built,' Miss Carstairs said. 'From there she could see right out across the fields behind

Tweeting Bottom and photograph any visiting birds. Her neighbours didn't like it much. They said it spoiled their view.'

Agatha and Randall left Tweeting Bottom a few minutes later. They drove in silence until they were on the road back to Mircester, Agatha enjoying the luxurious smooth ride of the big Mercedes. She'd never been particularly interested in cars. She was a wealthy woman and could certainly afford to buy a flashy car if she chose to, but she saw them as a necessity rather than a status symbol. It might be nice to sit in the more comfortable environment of a Mercedes like this when she was stuck for hours on a stakeout but, on the other hand, her unremarkable saloon car was far less noticeable. The last thing she needed on a covert job was someone admiring her car.

'So what did you think?' she said eventually. 'Anything of interest there?'

'Nothing much,' Randall said, sounding distinctly unimpressed. 'There were a couple of good modern cameras, but they don't fetch very high prices second hand. She had two nice old Zeiss cameras I think might go for a couple of hundred each and a 1930s Leica that could fetch over a thousand. I'll let my camera guy take a look at those. What about you? Anything you thought weird?'

'Not really, apart from the fact that they appear to be trying to offload all of Miss Feldrake's stuff before she's even cold.'

Agatha didn't entirely trust the smooth-talking Randall. He had lured her out of the office, confident that her curiosity wouldn't allow her to pass up on the invitation. That was a good word for Martin Randall, she thought to herself – confident. He was charming, good-looking and confident, yet he was also a schemer. She was pretty sure he could have sent his 'camera guy' to check out Miss Feldrake's collection. Instead, he'd used the trip to Tweeting Bottom as an excuse to see her – he'd admitted that much himself. What else did he have in mind?

'How about an early lunch?' he said cheerfully. 'I know a little pub not far from here and . . .'

There it was – as predictable as a three-minute egg.

'I don't think so, Martin,' she said, smiling politely. 'It's barely eleven o'clock and I need to get back to the office.'

'Of course you do,' he said. 'I know how busy you can be, but everyone has to eat at some time, don't they? So how about dinner instead?'

'I'm busy, Martin.'

'Ah, I see,' he said, her sterner tone putting not the slightest dink in the armour of his ego. 'Your dancing policeman has still got you under his thumb, hasn't he?'

Agatha's back stiffened. She looked across at him, her head tilted slightly to one side, her lips drawn as tight as a miser's purse.

'Nobody has me under their thumb,' she hissed. 'Not now – not ever! You'd do well to remember that!'

'Oh, come on, Agatha,' he said, the smile never leaving his bronzed features. 'Don't go getting upset.'

'You think this is upset?' she snarled, her temper building. 'You should see me when they put the wrong tonic in my gin! If you ever see me getting that upset, you'll need more than a perma-tan to hide behind! You're quite amazing, really, aren't you? They say men can't multi-task, yet here you are, breathing, talking, driving and being a complete arsehole all at the same time!'

He drew to a halt at some traffic lights not far from Mircester city centre.

'Don't be silly, Agatha,' Randall said. 'All I meant was—'

'Silly? *Silly?* I am *never* silly! That's another thing you'd do well to remember! I'll walk from here!' She got out and slammed the door. Mercedes doors, she noted with some satisfaction, slammed rather well.

When Agatha stormed back into the office, Helen Freedman was the first to notice that her temper was simmering. She offered a coffee, which Agatha politely accepted. Simon was out at the mall and Patrick was also out on a job. Toni looked up and immediately recognised the slight flush to her boss's cheeks and the white knuckles clutching her handbag as danger signs.

'Problem?' she asked.

'Just a pillock in a fancy car,' Agatha replied, allowing her shoulders to relax. 'No one I can't handle. Come into my office, Toni. Let's have a chat.'

Sitting behind her desk with a fresh cup of coffee, Agatha savoured the flavour. It was instant coffee, but it was Italian, it was expensive and she was fairly certain she could taste the slight sweetness of the Arabica beans. If she was fooling herself, she didn't much care. She liked it anyway.

'So what happened at Tweeting Bottom?' Toni asked.

'Well, I had a very interesting conversation with Mary Carstairs,' Agatha replied. 'It seems she and Anthony Feldrake are most definitely a couple – his wife has died so they're rekindling the flames of passion from their youth. Something was far from right there, though. Joan Feldrake seems to have been a very particular woman. She liked everything to be neat and tidy – everything in its place – yet it wasn't, not quite. I took a good look around and a couple of ornaments and picture frames on the living-room window ledge had been moved and not put back in quite the right place. You could tell by the marks where they had been protecting the paintwork from sun-fade over the years. It was the same with the furniture. There were marks in the carpet where every-thing had been moved, but not put back exactly in the same spot. It looked to me like the house had been very carefully searched.'

'Who would want to do that?' Toni asked. 'Feldrake and Carstairs?'

'Maybe,' Agatha mused, sipping her coffee, 'but it was his sister's house and it would seem they have unlimited access. He has every right to be there. Why would they have to be so careful about trying to put everything back just as it was? No, I got the distinct impression someone else had been in there.'

'Do you know if anything was missing?'

'That's impossible to tell, but there were plenty of desirable cameras in the place. If anyone was looking to make off with some easily transportable gear to sell, they'd definitely have gone for the cameras. No, the searching of the house is a real conundrum.'

'So is Anthony Feldrake,' Toni said, holding up her notebook. 'If his wife is dead, then I spent half an hour on the phone talking to a ghost this morning. Mrs Feldrake is very much alive – and looking forward to celebrating her divorce!'

Chapter Five

'Ah, Sergeant Wong – just the man!'

Bill Wong turned in the brashly lit, second-floor corridor of Mircester Police Station to see the gaunt figure of Detective Chief Inspector Wilkes striding towards him, his cheap, ill-fitting suit hanging on his gawky frame like a wet rag on a washing line.

'How can I help, sir?' Bill asked, tucking the paperwork he'd just picked up from a colleague into a buff folder. It was Tuesday morning, he'd just come on shift and he silently cursed his bad luck for having run into Wilkes so early.

'You're the one handling the accident near Ancombe, aren't you?' Wilkes said.

'Yes, sir. I was first on the scene, so it's fallen to me,' Bill replied.

'I know, I've seen your report,' Wilkes said. 'You'll be pleased to hear we're taking no further action.'

'No further action?' Bill was stunned. 'We haven't finished interviewing the people in the traffic queue, and the pathologist's report says—'

'Yes, yes, I've read that report, too.' Wilkes dismissed Bill's objections with a wave of his hand. 'There's nothing to concern us over the incident. We have too much else going on to waste time on some stupid woman who went walking in the woods after the most violent storm we've seen around here for years.'

'But the coroner will want to—' Bill began.

'There's no need for a coroner's inquiry,' Wilkes maintained. 'I have already confirmed that with the coroner.'

'Would that be when you played golf with him yesterday afternoon?' Bill said, eyeing Wilkes suspiciously.

'Don't you dare look at me like that, Sergeant!' Wilkes barked. 'And another thing: I see from your report that that bloody Raisin woman was at the scene. What was she doing there? You're friends with her, aren't you? All off for a nice outing together, were you?'

'Actually, it came as a complete surprise for me to see Mrs Raisin there,' Bill said. 'And I think there are some things about the incident that warrant further attention from us. The few statements we have taken so far don't quite add up and we need to get a team out there to conduct a proper search of the woods.'

'We don't have the manpower to waste on that!' Wilkes's voice was now bristling with anger. 'Shut down the inquiry and release the body to the family so they can arrange a funeral.'

'Sir, I really think that would be premature,' Bill protested.

'I don't care what you think!' Wilkes yelled, then leaned closer to Bill, wagging a warning finger. 'And don't you let Agatha Raisin go poking her nose in, or I'll stick you on permanent late shift for so long you won't have a bedtime story with that sprog of yours until it's visiting you in an old folks' home!'

Agatha was leaving for work that morning when she was surprised to see Doris Simpson walking up the front path.

'Good morning, Doris,' she said. 'You're early today.'

'I hope you don't mind, Mrs Raisin,' Doris said, 'but I promised my cousin Rita's daughter I'd help out at Carsely House at lunchtime, so I wanted an early start.'

'Rita's daughter is Zoe, isn't she?' Agatha said, the name popping into her head the way that the word 'twitchers' had failed to do. 'She's always dragging you into things. What has she got you doing this time?'

'Oh, it's just a spot of lunch for the old folks who live there,' Doris said, then laughed. 'Mind you, some of them aren't much older than me! We do them some snacks and sandwiches with tea or a small glass of wine now and again. It makes a change for them.'

'An old folks' home?' Agatha said, wrinkling her nose. 'Don't they all smell of boiled cabbage and stale wee?'

'Not Carsely House, Mrs Raisin,' Doris assured her. 'It's properly clean and modern nowadays. Anyway, we're planning to make lunch a bit of a garden party.'

'Well, you're certainly going to have the weather for it today,' Agatha said, looking up at a cloudless blue sky. 'It's hard to believe we were being battered by a storm just a few days ago.'

'That was terrible, weren't it? And what about Miss Feldrake? Tragic, weren't it?'

'It was. Did you know her well, Doris?'

'Not really,' Doris said. 'We was about the same age, maybe Joan Feldrake and the other two was a year younger, but a year means a lot when you're a teenager, don't it? Not so much nowadays, though. A year goes past in the blink of an eye!'

'You said they used to argue a lot.'

'Oh, yes, they was famous for it. I seen them screaming at each other in the Red Lion more than once.'

'What did they fall out about?'

'I can't rightly remember now,' Doris said, 'but if you're interested – and I think you asking questions means you're taking a proper interest – then I know someone who can tell you all about their bust-ups back in the day. She was the barmaid at the Red Lion.'

'Really? I'd like to meet her.'

'Why don't you come along to Carsely House at lunchtime, then? That's where she lives now. I'm sure she'll be happy to talk to you. She's in her eighties, but she's bright as a button. She loves a good natter, does old Elsie.'

Agatha agreed to meet Doris at Carsely House at 12.30 then set off for work, wondering what morsels of intrigue might be served up during lunch with the old folks.

When she arrived at Raisin Investigations, Toni and Patrick were chatting over a coffee at Toni's desk. Once she'd said 'good morning' to Mrs Freedman, Agatha joined them.

'Have you updated Patrick on Anthony Feldrake?' she asked.

'I was just about to,' Toni said, then turned to Patrick. 'Mary Carstairs told Agatha that Anthony's wife had died and that he had retired. It turns out, however, that Mrs Feldrake is very much alive and we now know that he didn't retire – he was sacked. Quite why he was sacked, we don't know. Mrs Feldrake either didn't know or wouldn't say. She wants nothing more to do with the man.'

'Where did he work?' Patrick asked.

'He was an engineer working on oil rigs being refurbished somewhere up in Scotland. Cromarty Firth is the place,' Toni replied, sounding a little uncertain.

'The Cromarty Firth sounds about right,' Patrick said, nodding. 'I've a Scottish friend who retired from the force and moved back north to live in Invergordon. I'll ask him to see what he can find out.'

'So we know we're being lied to,' Agatha said, 'but by whom? Mary Carstairs could simply be telling us what Feldrake told her.'

'On the other hand, she could be in on the lies,' Toni pointed out, 'in order to cover for him.'

'Quite,' Agatha said, 'although if she was faking the tears that appeared when she spoke to me, then she put on quite a performance. We need to find out more about Miss Carstairs and her two twitcher friends, which is why you and I are going on a special mission at lunchtime to Carsely House, Toni.'

'The old folks' home?' Toni said, looking slightly aghast. 'Don't they all smell of—'

'Not Carsely House,' Agatha broke in, wagging her finger. 'It's all thoroughly modern and, in any case, we'll be attending a garden party – so we'll be outside.'

Carsely House was a large, stone manor house on the outskirts of the village. It wasn't somewhere Agatha had ever visited before, mainly because it was tucked away out of sight, neither on the way to somewhere nor on the way from anywhere. It was also a retirement home – not a place in which she'd ever had cause to take an interest. She'd always been amazed at how many titbits of information she could pick up in the Red Lion, and she'd occasionally heard people in the pub talking about Carsely House. They referred to it as 'God's Waiting Room', 'Bedpan Alley' or 'The Farewell Inn'. She was pleasantly surprised, therefore, when they arrived there that afternoon and the place actually looked rather attractive.

The main building was a Victorian country house with a sunny aspect, surrounded by well-tended lawns, with flower beds close to the house. Beyond the lawns, shrubberies gave way to trees, providing shelter and privacy for the building. The house was two storeys high and the large, multi-paned windows had immaculately painted white frames. Judging by the number of windows – far fewer than Sir Charles's sprawling Barfield House, where she had never been able to count all of the windows (Charles maintained that there were, mysteriously, more windows visible on the outside than you could count when you visited the rooms) – Agatha guessed there were no more than ten bedrooms.

That level of accommodation didn't seem to tally with the number of people who were sitting at garden tables arranged randomly on a wide patio and a flat area of lawn. There was a parking area to one side of the house and Doris Simpson came rushing towards them as they stepped out of the car.

'Oh, thank goodness you're here, Mrs Raisin,' Doris said, sounding flustered. 'And you've brought Miss Gilmour, too. Even better. Two of Zoe's usual helpers have called in sick. Would you mind giving us a hand offering round sandwiches and suchlike?'

'Act like a waitress?' Agatha said, sounding somewhat appalled.

'It would be such a help,' Doris implored her. 'Some of the real crotchety ones get grouchy if others are being served and they have to wait.'

'Of course we'll help,' Toni said, nudging Agatha.

'Yes ... we can hand out sandwiches,' Agatha said, with some reluctance. She and Toni followed Doris towards the house. 'There seem to be more residents than can possibly fit in the building.'

'Not all of them live in the main building,' Doris explained, leading them into a reception area that would not have looked out of place in a four-star hotel. 'There's a newer area of terraced bungalows out the back and some small lodges in the woods for married couples. It's all very nice here, you know.'

They passed a couple of tastefully furnished lounge areas before arriving in the kitchen, which was of industrial proportion but spotlessly clean in stainless steel and aluminium. Even here, Agatha noted with huge relief, there was not the slightest whiff of boiled cabbage – or anything even less fragrant – in the air. Zoe was on her way out to the garden with a loaded tray and Doris pointed out two other trays, laden with sandwiches and snacks, sitting waiting to go.

'If you could take one each,' Doris said, 'I'll bring out the last one, then Zoe and I should be able to manage from there on.'

'Which one is Elsie the barmaid?' Agatha asked, pausing at the door to the garden.

'She's in her wheelchair at the table with the yellow sunshade on the right,' Doris said, 'and thank you, Mrs Raisin. You're a lifesaver.'

Agatha nodded and set off to save some lives with tuna-mayonnaise sandwiches, mini sausage rolls and a variety of other savoury delights. By the time she had meandered between tables all the way to where Elsie was sitting, she had only one sandwich left. Elsie looked up at her. Had Agatha not known how old she was, she'd have placed her at least twenty years younger. Her long hair fell in silver-grey waves to her shoulders and her make-up was expertly applied, bringing a glow to her skin that made any wrinkles struggle to make their presence felt. Although her glamorous looks were fading in her twilight years, Agatha decided that Elsie must have been a real head-turner in her youth.

'Thank you, Mrs Raisin,' Elsie said.

'You know who I am,' Agatha said, a little surprised.

'I've lived around Carsely all my life,' Elsie said, then laughed, letting the wrinkles play around her mouth and eyes. 'Well, almost all – I'm not dead yet! I get to hear all the gossip. I only *hear* it now, of course. When I were a bit younger, I used to *be* all the gossip!'

She laughed again, a joyous, infectious cackle that left Agatha with no option but to join in.

'So, I know who you are, Mrs Raisin,' Elsie said, giving Agatha a wink that appeared to mean she had met with Elsie's approval. Toni then appeared with a much depleted tray.

'Would you like a slice of quiche?' she offered.

'Did Mrs Raisin make it?' asked Elsie.

'No, I didn't,' said Agatha.

'Should be safe to give it a try, then!' Elsie said, rocking with laughter again.

Toni tried hard not to laugh, failed and turned away in order not to catch Agatha's eye. Agatha, now abundantly aware that Elsie knew far more about her – including the poisoned quiche incident from quite some time ago – than she knew about Elsie, remained stony-faced.

'So what do you two want?' Elsie asked, calming herself.

'What do you mean?' Agatha responded.

'I'm sitting here on my own because Doris said you might like to have a word. You've never shown any interest in me or this place before, so for you to show up here asking for me, you must be up to something. What's it all about?'

'I think you should be working for me as a detective, Elsie,' Agatha said, gently settling into a garden chair not dissimilar to those in Margaret Bloxby's garden.

'Why would I want to work for you, Mrs Raisin, when you're here, serving my lunch, working for me?' The old lady laughed again.

'We heard you used to work at the Red Lion,' Toni said, also taking a seat.

'That were fifty-odd years ago,' Elsie confirmed, shaking her head. 'Fifty years, would you believe it?'

'We need to find out a bit about three young women who used to go there – Stella Smart, Mary Carstairs and Joan Feldrake,' Agatha said. 'Do you remember them?'

'Oh, I knew them all right,' Elsie confirmed, and sighed. 'Joan got herself killed the other day, didn't she? Proper shame that were. I remember those three when they was just teenagers, probably a year or so underage to be drinking in the pub, but old Joe, who ran the place back then, didn't bother too much about that. Having girls in the pub meant that boys would come in and buy them drinks. It was good for business.'

'The Red Lion's my local,' Agatha said. 'It's a good village pub, but it's never seemed like a place for young people.'

'Ah, but things were different back then, Mrs Raisin,' Elsie said, waving a finger in the air as though winding back time. 'The housing estate out the back of Carsely had just been built and there were plenty of youngsters looking for somewhere to hang out. Joan, Stella and Mary didn't come from the estate, though. They were Mircester Grammar School girls. They lived in the posh houses off the Mircester road. They'd come in trying to act all sophisticated and order Cointreau with lemonade. Joe always told me to make sure they didn't have too much. Once a week there was a disco, or a live band. We even had that Stevie Sexton in there once.'

'Stevie Sexton?' Toni sounded sceptical. 'Didn't he

have hits with "Loving All Night Long" and "Wake Me When It's Over"?'

'That's the very man!' Elsie said, laughing, 'but you're too young – how come you know about him?'

'My . . . er . . . mum used to like him,' Toni said, with a slight hesitation.

'Ah, bless you, my dear, for trying to be kind and not make an old lady feel quite so old,' Elsie said, 'but I doubt your mum were even born when those songs were hits. Stevie Sexton would have been your granny's favourite! He died a couple of years back, couple of days after Burt Bacharach. Of course, Sexton were only in the bar because of Mary Carstairs.'

'A pop star was interested in Miss Carstairs?' Agatha could scarcely believe her ears.

'Not as such,' Elsie explained, 'although Mary was a looker, all right. She wasn't after Sexton, but those other two was besotted with him. That's why Mary got him to come to the pub.'

'She tried to set one of the others up with Stevie Sexton?' Toni was intrigued.

'Actually, the very opposite,' Elsie said, bursting out laughing again. 'Mary had a part-time job at Mircester Theatre. Fancied herself as a bit of an actress, but nothing ever came of that. She worked in the office. When Stevie Sexton did a few shows there, she told him that the Red Lion in Carsely was a good place to pick up girls.

'Well, the pub was busy the night he walked in and a lot of young ladies, even those with boyfriends, was squealing and rushing up for autographs. It calmed down after a bit, but Mary was standing at the bar with

104

Stella and Joan. Those two was so excited I thought they was going to wet themselves. Sexton never spoke to them. Didn't even notice them. About half an hour later, he walked out with a blonde on each arm. Stella and Joan looked like their whole world had just fallen apart.

'Mary, on the other hand, was over the moon. She laughed in their faces. She knew they weren't his type. Joan was quite glam, with loads of long dark hair, but Stella was too plain for the likes of him. Mary took great delight in telling them that, when he was playing the theatre, he had different girls every night and he'd never look twice at the likes of them!'

'Nasty . . .' Agatha said, looking confused. 'I thought those three were friends. That's not how friends behave. Why did Mary do that?'

'Because they was always at each other's throats, Mrs Raisin,' Elsie explained. 'It's probably why they stuck together. Everyone knew what they was like, so nobody else wanted them as friends. The Stevie Sexton thing came after a prank they roped me in on.'

'Really?' Toni said. 'How come you got involved?'

'Stella and Joan offered me ten quid,' Elsie said, and snorted. 'Wouldn't buy more than a couple of drinks these days, but back then that was nearly a week's wages for me.'

'What did they want you to do?' Agatha asked.

'Joan had a brother, Anthony, who was a couple of years older. They wanted me to give him a kiss. I couldn't believe it. A week's wages for one little kiss round the back of the pub? I'd have been mad to turn that down. I didn't know him. I thought he must have been some sad kid who'd never kissed a girl, so I agreed.

105

'Well, I didn't find out until afterwards, but Mary had a real crush on Anthony, and he was apparently pretty keen on her, too. Stella and Joan didn't have boyfriends and Joan definitely didn't want Mary going out with her brother, so they offered me ten quid to kiss Anthony. Stella and Joan, of course, made sure that Mary saw me snogging Anthony. She was heartbroken. He went off to do some sort of apprenticeship soon after and Mary never did find another boyfriend. I don't think any of them did, but I felt sorry for Mary.'

'If it makes you feel any better, Elsie,' Agatha said, 'I can tell you that Mary and Anthony have got back together.'

'They have?' Elsie said, looking genuinely pleased. 'If you see them, Mrs Raisin, tell them I'm sorry – about what I did and about what happened to Joan – and I'm happy for them.'

Agatha and Toni chatted with Elsie for a little longer, then said their goodbyes and headed for the car. Toni clipped her seatbelt into place and looked across at Agatha behind the wheel.

'A week's wages just for one kiss?' Toni said.

'You're not my type,' Agatha said.

'No, I meant—'

'Yes I know what you meant, Toni. That was just my little joke,' Agatha said, starting the engine.

'Yes, but if somebody offered me a week's—'

'Don't forget you're talking to your boss here, Toni,' Agatha said, smiling. 'I know what I pay you and that would be a very expensive kiss!'

'Exactly.' Toni nodded. 'The temptation would be just

to go for it. What's one little kiss, after all? But nothing's ever as simple as that, is it? I'd be thinking that there has to be a catch.'

'When it comes to men, Toni, there's always a catch,' Agatha agreed, heading for the main road. 'But the most important thing we learned from old Elsie was that Mary Carstairs was an actress – so were the grief and tears I saw real or were they Miss Carstairs' bid for an Oscar?'

Back at Raisin Investigations, Patrick had come up with some intriguing insights into life in Tweeting Bottom.

'A mate of mine at the local council says that Joan Feldrake's neighbours complained about her birdwatching hide,' he reported.

'I've seen it,' Agatha said. 'Apparently they were unhappy about it spoiling their view.'

'Because the hide didn't actually contravene any regulations,' Patrick said, 'there wasn't much the council could do about it, but Feldrake's neighbours carried on complaining and the council did get involved to try to calm everything down. Nothing was resolved, and the hide remained in place, but the neighbours suddenly stopped complaining. At one point there were phone calls, emails and letters to the council on an almost daily basis and then, strangely, nothing at all.'

'Maybe they just gave up,' Toni suggested.

'They didn't seem like the sort who would just throw in the towel,' Patrick said. 'In some of their messages, they swore they'd fight on for as long as it took to get rid of what they referred to as "the eyesore".'

'Disputes between neighbours can get heated,' Agatha said, considering how the hostility might have escalated, 'but would it be enough to kill someone over?'

'Are we even sure Joan Feldrake was murdered?' Patrick said. 'Everything points to her death being an accident.'

'I think there's more to it than that,' Agatha said, 'and I want to get to the bottom of it.'

'You're the boss,' Patrick said, a rare smile brightening his craggy features, 'and you've been right about these things in the past.'

'So we'll keep on this,' Agatha said. 'Tweeting Bottom seems such a peaceful little place. Anything more on the neighbours?'

'Only that Joan Feldrake complained about her other neighbour, Eric Spalding,' Patrick continued. 'She objected to him making so much noise with his music and blocking the road when he parked his van there. The council threatened to confiscate his amplifiers and speakers. He then threatened Joan Feldrake and the police got involved. He was given a caution. That was over a year ago.'

'So, Joan Feldrake had problems with her neighbours,' Toni began, counting off points on her fingers. 'She had problems with her two best friends. Her brother has lied and seems keen to cash in on her property. Then, of course, there's Guy Fawkes.'

'You know,' Agatha said, letting Toni's list settle in her mind, 'for someone who may not have been murdered, Joan Feldrake's death is throwing up a whole host of murder suspects. Toni, we need to know more about her neighbours. I've been seen in Tweeting Bottom, so you need to make up some pretext for going door-to-door there asking questions. Patrick, I know you're busy with lots of other things, but anything more you can find out on Stella Smart and Mary Carstairs would be good. I'll concentrate on Guy Fawkes . . . and here's just the man to help me with that.'

Roy Silver walked into the office, wearing dusky pink chinos and a primrose checked shirt.

'Help you with what?' he asked.

'You can come with me on a little trip to Barfield House,' Agatha said, 'in pursuit of our inquiries.'

'Fabulous, darling!' Roy cooed. 'I've arrived just in time. Things must be getting serious if you're visiting Sir Charles Fraith!'

The avenue of rhododendrons leading from Barfield House's ornate gates up to the building itself had but a few blooms remaining from their spring splendour, although the foliage cast a welcome cool shade across the drive. When the old house drifted into view it was, as always, both impressive and uninspiring. It was impressive because of its sheer size, yet uninspiring due to its gloomy demeanour. Even in the sunshine it managed to look wearily depressed, the many windows in their dark frames failing miserably to raise its spirits.

'It's a funny old pile, isn't it?' said Roy as they parked on the gravel near the steps leading up to the entrance.

'By funny, I think you mean strange,' Agatha said. 'If it were funny, it would put a smile on your face each time you saw it, and it never does that.'

'No,' Roy agreed. 'It's the sort of house that needs a kick in the arse and to be told to cheer up.'

The huge oak door opened before they reached the final stone step and Gustav, Sir Charles's loyal manservant, stood on the threshold. Gustav had been butler to Sir Charles's father and had continued to work at Barfield House through thick and thin, as butler, chauffer, gardener, handyman and cook when times had been hard. In the past, he had been a stalwart ally to Agatha in defence of Sir Charles. Yet, when the dust settled, he always reverted to type, and his type regarded people from most walks of life, including some minor aristocrats, as simply being beneath them. Agatha's past relationship with Sir Charles had been all but unbearable for Gustav.

'Oh, it's you ...' he said, glaring at Agatha from beneath dark brows before slowly shifting target to Roy, '... and him.'

'Stop messing about, Gustav,' Agatha said. 'I phoned ahead. We're expected.'

'I believe you are, Mrs Raisin,' Gustav conceded, 'although there remains a world of difference between "expected" and "welcome".'

'As gracious as ever,' Agatha said, patting Gustav's cheek as she breezed past. 'Keep smiling, Gustav.'

Roy followed, started to say something, then felt Gustav's glower hit him like a hammer blow and hurried on. Agatha led the way to the library, Sir Charles's favourite room, where she knew he would be sitting behind his vast desk, shuffling papers and poring over spreadsheets.

110

'Aggie, sweetie!' Charles beamed at her as soon as she stepped into the bright, spacious room. The ceiling was high and the wall opposite the door was devoted mainly to windows and French doors looking out over the terrace and the landscaped grounds beyond. To Agatha's right and left, the walls were lined with bookshelves housing a vast collection of volumes both ancient and modern. Like the windows on the outside of the house, whenever Agatha had tried to count them, she'd lost interest long before she could work out exactly how many books there were. Charles had once told her there were 'somewhere around three thousand', although he'd neither counted them nor ever intended to attempt to read them all. If there was any book on the shelf that advised on how best to greet Agatha Raisin, he had certainly never read it.

'How many times do I have to tell you not to call me that?' Agatha asked him, her lips set in a thin line. 'It's Agatha, not "Aggie", and I am not your "sweetie", but since you know not to use either of those terms, I suppose I have to assume you did so in order to wind me up. Well, I refuse to be antagonized.'

'Quite right, too,' Charles said, approaching her with open arms for an affectionate hug. He was a small man with fine, fair hair and a sensitive face. Gustav ensured that his shirts were always as crisply immaculate as the day they left London's Jermyn Street and that his suits were as superbly pristine as the day his Savile Row tailor last whisked a brush over them. 'Old habits, you know, but we're much too dear to each other to fall out over my little transgressions. I see you've brought Roy along. Come in and sit down, old chap.'

Charles ushered Agatha and Roy to oversized, outrageously comfortable armchairs near the ornate fireplace. No fire burned in the grate but fresh logs were stacked there, ready to host a fireside chat over brandy when the evenings turned cooler. Agatha looked over to a wingback chair by the terrace windows where Charles's aged aunt, Mrs Tassy, sat in the perfect spot to enjoy enough natural light to read her book, but to avoid any bothersome sunshine giving her eye strain. She wore her customary dark, high-necked dress and looked up from reading to study Agatha with her watery blue eyes. She gave the hint of a smile and nodded a greeting which Agatha returned. The old woman looked, and sometimes acted, like a relic from a bygone age, but she and Agatha had developed a degree of mutual respect over the years. Having acknowledged Agatha's presence, Mrs Tassy returned to her book.

'Now, what was it you wanted to talk to me about?' Charles asked, seating himself on a couch and shooing away Gustav, who was fussing around them folding a newspaper from the coffee table and flicking imaginary dust with a white cloth which, like a stage magician, he had produced from nowhere.

'Someone who has become a person of interest in an ongoing investigation,' Agatha said, glad that Charles had cut to the chase. 'We think he might be one of your tenant farmers. His name is Fawkes.'

'Ah, yes, Gethin Fawkes,' said Charles. 'He's not actually one of my tenants. His land is just beyond the estate, but I know exactly who you mean. Actually, I've been in touch with him a few times recently. I offered to buy a parcel of his land when we were planning the vineyard. Claudette thought it would have been perfect.'

Claudette Duvivier was Agatha's friend. She ran her own vineyard in France and had been advising Charles on growing vines and the development of the Chateau Barfield business.

'I take it Mr Fawkes didn't want to sell?' Roy asked.

'No, and he was adamant that he would never sell any of his land. Turned a bit aggressive when I tried to push him – you know, negotiate a bit,' Charles explained. 'I backed off after that. Over the years, I've heard a few stories about our Mr Fawkes and his explosive temper.'

'Explosive? That word conjures up all sorts of thoughts,' Agatha said, raising her eyebrows. 'Gethin Fawkes isn't related to Guy Fawkes, the one who tried to blow up Parliament, is he? It's a pretty unusual surname, after all.'

'An interesting name, certainly,' Charles agreed. 'Obviously I did as much research as I could on Mr Fawkes before I approached him . . .'

'As much as you could without calling me in,' Agatha noted. 'Background checks are a major part of our business, you know.'

'It wasn't that big a deal, Aggie . . . atha,' Charles said. He caught the look in Agatha's eye and quickly moved on. 'I think you were busy with that Bowling Green Murder. I thought I was capable of doing a bit of ferreting around. I do have—'

'I know – a First in history from Cambridge,' Agatha said, rolling her eyes.

'I wasn't going to say that. All I meant was that I do have a bit of common sense.'

'Okay, so what did your common sense and your history degree tell you about Fawkes?'

'In fact, I knew him from many years ago when I used to go to some of the local Young Farmers' events,' Charles said. 'Fawkes didn't really mix much, and some of the chaps used to make fun of him by calling him Guido. I think he only went to those parties to please his father.'

'His father died when he was just a little boy, you know,' came the reedy voice of Mrs Tassy.

'Gethin Fawkes?' asked Roy.

'No, Guy Fawkes,' said Mrs Tassy. 'He was one of the Yorkshire Fawkeses.'

'I didn't realise you were so interested in history, Mrs Tassy,' Agatha said.

'You don't get to my age without picking up a thing or two, Mrs Raisin,' Mrs Tassy said, closing her book. 'I've lived through a lot of what the schools teach as history nowadays. My grandfather thought it was funny that he served in the First War with a major in the Yorkshire Hussars called Freddy Fawkes who claimed to be related to Guy Fawkes. Freddy went on to become a Member of Parliament – working in the very place that his ancestor had tried to blow up! I remember that!'

'The Gunpowder Plot was more than four hundred years ago,' Gustav said. 'Surely even you can't remember that far back.'

'That's quite enough, Gustav,' Charles said. 'Perhaps you might fetch us some tea.'

'I'll have Mrs Roberts bring it in,' Gustav grunted. 'She can probably find the library by now if I point her in the right direction.'

114

'Mrs Roberts?' Agatha asked. 'Who's Mrs Roberts?'

'A rather confused woman Charles saw fit to employ as a housemaid,' said Mrs Tassy with a sigh.

'She's the wife of a former estate worker who has . . . um . . . rather fallen on hard times,' Charles explained.

'Her husband ran off with the postman,' Mrs Tassy said in a matter-of-fact tone. 'Apparently they now have a smallholding together in New Zealand. The Fawkeses kept zebras on their estate in Yorkshire, you know. I always admired that idea.'

'Zebras? Really?' said Roy. 'How lovely!'

'Why would they . . .? No, never mind that,' said Agatha. 'None of that's helping me to get to know our Mr Fawkes. I need to pay him a visit.'

'I can help you with that,' Charles said, and crossed the room to his desk where he picked up his phone, dialled a number and waited. 'Gethin? Yes, it's Charles, old boy . . . No, I'm not going to badger you about that field. I need a favour from you. A friend of mine is helping . . .'

Charles paused, realising that he hadn't thought through a cover story for Agatha.

'A writer research a novel . . .?' Roy suggested.

Charles relayed that down the phone then looked up for more inspiration.

'And needs to find out about farming sheep,' Roy prompted.

Charles passed on Roy's subterfuge, agreed with Fawkes that they could visit the following morning providing that he didn't pester Fawkes for the land ever again, then hung up just as Mrs Roberts arrived with the

115

tea. Agatha studied her as she crossed the room to set the tray down on the coffee table.

Mrs Roberts looked to be in her late thirties, far younger than Agatha was expecting, although she had no idea why she'd been expecting someone older. She had a mass of wavy reddish-blonde hair tied back in an unruly ponytail, a pale, pretty face and the fulsome figure of the kind of woman with whom Charles had cheated on Agatha more times than she cared to remember.

'Do let me give you a hand with that, Mrs Roberts,' Charles said, leaping to his feet a little too late to be of any real assistance, but not so late as to miss the opportunity to gently lay his hand on hers. She pulled her hand away.

'Actually, it's Miss MacNeil,' she said.

'Not until your divorce comes through, young lady,' Mrs Tassy reminded her. 'Until then you're still Mrs Roberts.'

Mrs Roberts tutted and stalked out of the room. Charles watched her go, then turned to his aunt.

'Did you have to be so blunt?' he said. 'You've upset her now.'

'I find the truth is rarely as upsetting as pretence and duplicity,' she replied.

'I should go and check on her,' Charles said and hurried off, leaving a momentary silence hanging in the air that was eventually broken by Roy.

'Have you ever met Gethin Fawkes, Mrs Tassy?' he asked.

'Not personally,' she replied, removing her reading glasses, 'but I do know the sad story about his poor wife.

Her family farmed in Wales and their cattle all had to be exterminated during the foot-and-mouth epidemic back in 2001.'

'Exterminated,' Agatha mused. 'That's not a word you hear very often.'

'Thankfully not,' said Mrs Tassy, 'but Mrs Fawkes had been brought up on stories about diseases that could be spread to livestock by people and fretted incessantly about hikers tromping over their fields. Worry and stress made her very ill and she eventually died of heart failure.'

'That could explain why Fawkes doesn't like trespassers,' Roy said.

'I think it explains precisely why he doesn't like trespassers,' Mrs Tassy agreed.

Deciding that their mission was accomplished, Agatha suggested it was time to leave. She and Roy bumped into Gustav in the hall, where he had clearly been lurking.

'Leaving so soon?' he said.

'Surely I can never leave soon enough for you, Gustav?' Agatha replied.

'Actually, there's something I wanted to mention . . .' Gustav said, looking distinctly uncomfortable. 'We've worked together in Sir Charles's best interests in the past and . . .'

'Don't tell me,' Agatha said. 'You're worried about him and Mrs Roberts.'

'Quite,' Gustav said. 'She seems to be taking a lot of his attention. I don't really know what he sees in her.'

'She's an attractive woman, Gustav,' Agatha pointed out. 'I think it's obvious what he sees in her.'

'It's not that,' Gustav said. 'There's more to it than that.'

'Well, if you find out what it is,' Agatha said, 'do let me know. On second thoughts, don't bother. I really couldn't care less.'

With that, she and Roy made their way out to her car.

Their departure was observed from the library by Mrs Tassy, with Charles standing at her shoulder.

'What is this little game you're playing, Charles?' she asked her nephew.

'It's no game, Aunt,' he replied. 'It's a strategy – a masterplan.'

'If it involves trying to trick your way back into Mrs Raisin's affections,' she warned him, 'you're playing with fire.'

'Agatha Raisin always wants what she can't have,' Charles said with a smile. 'Maybe if it looks like I'm becoming unattainable, she'll start taking an interest again.'

'Be very careful, Charles,' said the old lady. 'Agatha Raisin is not a woman to be trifled with.'

Chapter Six

As the afternoon wore on towards the end of the day, around the time when office workers start thinking of heading home, wondering what to have for dinner and what to watch on telly, Agatha was sifting through some paperwork on her desk, trying to remember if she still had a lasagne in her freezer, or if she had finished all of her frozen ready meals the previous week.

She had almost decided to call in at Harvey's, Carsely's post-office-cum-general-store, on her way home for one of her periodic raids on their freezer section, when John appeared in the office.

'I wasn't expecting to see you,' she said, rounding her desk to give him a peck on the cheek. 'I thought you were in Southampton again.'

'I got away earlier than expected,' he said, grinning and holding her in his arms, 'so I made a chicken casserole when I got home. Fancy dinner at my place and a turn around the dance floor?'

He spun her round, the closest they could get to dancing in the cramped space to the side of her huge desk. John had built a small studio in his back garden with a dance floor just big enough for him to give

private lessons. They had spent many romantic evenings together drifting round the floor in their very own
mini-ballroom.

'That sounds like a wonderful idea,' she said, all
thoughts of Harvey's melting away like the frost on a
frozen shepherd's pie.

'Can't have too late a night, though,' he said, stretch-
ing his neck wearily. 'I'm feeling a bit tired and we've
another training session to get through with the ship's
entertainment staff tomorrow.'

'I promise not to wear you out completely,' she said,
laughing. Then she spotted Bill Wong crossing the outer
office. 'My goodness! An afternoon's boring paperwork
and then not one but two handsome men show up. How
lucky can a girl get?'

Bill smiled pleasantly, then closed the door behind
him, although only Helen Freedman was in the outer
office and she was putting on her coat, ready to catch her
bus home to Evesham.

'I need to have a word with you, Agatha,' he said.

'Sounds serious,' Agatha replied, returning to her
chair. John took the only other seat, Bill declining it when
offered, preferring to remain standing, although leaning
on the doorpost.

'Not too serious,' he said, 'but DCI Wilkes has told
me to warn you not to get mixed up in the death of Joan
Feldrake. As far as he's concerned, the case is closed.
Miss Feldrake's body is being released to her brother
tomorrow and her belongings will also be given to him
then. That will be the end of the matter as far as Mircester
Police are concerned.'

'Wilkes is a fool,' said John. 'Even if that poor woman's death was an accident, your guys can't have gone through all the proper procedures in only three days!'

'I would rather do things differently,' Bill said, shrugging. 'There are some loose ends about the case that I think need to be investigated, but it's not up to me.'

'Why does Wilkes think I'll get involved?' Agatha asked.

'Because he knows you were there – that much is in my initial report,' Bill explained, 'and he doesn't want you looking into things that he's prepared to let slide.'

'So there are things about the case that give cause for concern?' Agatha asked.

'I can't really discuss that,' Bill said. 'My orders were to make sure you knew that any inquiries you might choose to make would be frowned upon. I would be in big trouble if I passed on any information to you or anyone from Raisin Investigations.'

Bill then said goodbye and reached out to shake hands with John before leaving the office.

'That was all very strange,' Agatha said, shaking her head. 'It was most unlike Bill.'

'Was it?' John said, chuckling. 'He'd be in trouble if he gave details about the case to you or your team, but *I'm* not on your payroll.' John opened his hand to reveal a small sliver of grey plastic – a computer SD card.

'Bill gave you that just now?' Agatha asked, and John nodded. 'Clever boy. If anyone should ask, he can truthfully say that he didn't hand over anything to me or my team. Let's see what's on it.'

Agatha slotted the card into a port on the laptop

computer sitting on her desk and John joined her to view the screen. She scrolled through several documents, each many pages long.

'That looks like Bill's report, the pathologist's report, statements from the paramedics and a few other witness statements – Anthony Feldrake, Mary Carstairs and Stella Smart.'

'All good stuff,' John said, 'but a lot to read through.'

'You're right,' Agatha said, removing the card and closing her laptop. 'Chicken casserole and a slow foxtrot are calling. This can wait.'

It waited only until Agatha arrived home later that night. She fed the cats, poured herself a glass of wine and sat down with her laptop. She started with Bill's report, but after fewer than three minutes reading she stopped, tutted and got up to fetch a notepad and pen. Clearly, there was going to be a slew of anomalies that needed further explanation and she was going to have to make a list.

In the Raisin Investigations office the following morning, Agatha's team gathered around her desk. She asked Simon for the first update, since he was due back at the shopping mall imminently. He looked even more disreputable than he had on Monday morning.

'Well, I've seen how the shoplifters operate,' he said, shaking his head, 'and for what looks like a bunch of wasted crackheads, they're actually really well organised.'

'What do you mean?' Agatha asked.

'I've seen them arriving at the mall,' Simon went on, 'and they're clever about how they do things. They show up with a plan. There are sometimes half a dozen of them, sometimes up to ten. One or two of them might be dressed in decent clothes and have cleaned themselves up a bit. That way the store security guys don't always recognise them straight away. They never go in when it's quiet. They wait until lunchtime when there are lots of people in the shops. That's when they start filtering into the mall, one at a time or in pairs.

'They'll then set up a couple of diversions – an argument with a check-out clerk or a staged fight between a couple of them – and that's when the thieves will hit the chosen stores. They take things that are easy to pocket – jewellery, perfume, even posh chocolate – then they all leave by different exits. There are so many ways out of that place – through the car park or out onto the high street or at least three different side streets – that they're generally gone before anyone realises something's been nicked.'

'What do they do with all the stuff?' Toni asked.

'I've tailed a couple of them,' Simon said. 'The security guys can't do that. They have to stay in the mall. Apparently it would cause all sorts of legal problems if they tried grabbing the scumbags in the street, especially if they caught up with the ones who didn't have any goods on them. I followed them down to the old cathedral – the bit where the ruined walls are. They met a bloke there who took whatever they had and paid them in drugs. Everything has a value, and I heard them arguing – negotiating, I suppose – over "Golden Girl", "Special K" and "501s".'

'Serious stuff,' Agatha said, nodding. 'I know "Golden Girl" is heroin and "Special K" is ketamine, but I'm not sure about . . . what was it? . . . "501s"—'

'Crack cocaine,' Patrick cut in. 'How are these people even able to operate? They must be off their heads most of the time.'

'It's not always the same crew,' Simon explained. 'I think there's a hard core of ringleaders but the minor players change all the time. And it's not just the mall they're hitting. I've seen them coming out of the big department stores in the high street – pretty much anywhere they can mingle with a shopping crowd.'

'Any photos of this Fagin character who handles the stolen goods?' Agatha asked.

'Sorry, boss, but I can't get close enough without being spotted,' Simon apologised. 'My phone gets nothing when I try to zoom in and I can't carry a big camera.'

'Try this,' Agatha said, reaching into a desk drawer to retrieve a package. 'I sent for it the other day. It's a monocular. You can carry it in a pocket and clip it to your phone for long-range shots. Don't take any risks, though, Simon. If you can get a picture or two, we'll hand them over to the mall management with our report and recommend that they call in Mircester Police.'

'Cool,' Simon said, examining the monocular. 'I'll give it a go.'

He then left to prepare for another day at the mall and Patrick offered his findings on Joan Feldrake.

'She worked for a number of years as a bookkeeper

at a Mircester accountancy firm, Boddington's,' he said. 'According to my contact at Mircester Chamber of Commerce, she even had some shares in the company. When a couple of Boddington's original directors decided to retire, they offered their shares for sale to other shareholders. Joan bought some and the rest were eventually acquired by Stella Smart, who had been left shares by her aunt many years before. Feldrake then sold all her shares to Smart, who ended up as the company's major shareholder – basically, she took over. Feldrake then had enough in the bank to retire early.

'The guys running the company, Keith Boddington and his cousin, Alan Trimble, were furious. They'd lost control of their family business. Stella Smart then started pushing for changes and milking every penny she could out of the place. She's not at all popular with Boddington and Trimble, and neither was Joan Feldrake.'

'Hmm ...' Agatha pondered the information. 'Yet more potential suspects with a grudge against Joan Feldrake. See if you can find a way to set up a meeting with Boddington and Trimble, Patrick. Who'd have thought one middle-aged spinster from cosy little Tweeting Bottom could have so many enemies?'

'Speaking of Tweeting Bottom,' Toni said, holding up a lanyard with a photo identity card attached. 'I'm heading there this morning. I'm a university social anthropology researcher asking about relationships between neighbours in rural communities.'

Toni was wearing a plain white T-shirt, very short denim shorts and running shoes. Agatha gave her a look that verged on disapproval.

'You're going dressed like that?' she said.

'I have to look the part,' Toni said, unfolding a pair of large spectacles and placing them on her face before picking up a blue clipboard. 'And in my bag I have my phone, lipstick and a can of UK-legal pepper spray alternative.'

'Phone in after every call,' Agatha said, 'and stay safe. Doorstep only. Don't go inside. You can count on someone watching you all the time you're in Tweeting Bottom, but you can't count on anyone coming to help if you get in trouble. Be on your guard at every doorstep.'

Toni nodded and Agatha reached for her notebook.

'I have a few things from the official reports on Joan Feldrake's death that don't make sense. The first is that Stella Smart claims she was sent a message saying a magnolia warbler had been spotted, but she doesn't know who sent it. Anthony Feldrake and Mary Carstairs say Joan also received that message.'

'Is that so unusual?' Patrick asked. 'Word about a rare sighting must flash through the birdwatching fraternity pretty quickly.'

'I'm sure it does,' Agatha agreed. 'So why were there no other twitchers there? Did Mary Carstairs get the message? Why wasn't she there with Feldrake and Smart? She says meeting Joan Feldrake at the Feathers was more important to her, but I'm not so sure. Our three twitchers would all have been very competitive about catching sight of a rare bird. A couple of phone calls early this morning confirmed that no other local birdwatching groups knew anything about a magnolia warbler in the area. In fact, they were extremely dubious

126

about the alleged sighting. We need to know who sent those messages.'

'You think Miss Feldrake and Miss Smart were lured there? It was some kind of trap?' Toni asked.

'Could be,' said Patrick. 'Or Smart lured Feldrake, but even if it was a trap, how do you kill someone by making a tree fall on them?'

'The pathologist's report,' Agatha said, sliding some papers across the desk for her colleagues to see. 'There were fragments of tree bark in Feldrake's head wound. The bark was from an oak tree, but the tree she was lying under was a beech.'

Patrick read the relevant lines in the report, then pushed it aside.

'I've seen big trees come down,' he said. 'They bring branches and debris with them from other trees round about. The beech tree could have had an oak branch tangled up in it.'

'Maybe,' said Toni, 'or maybe somebody whacked Miss Feldrake with an oak tree branch, then laid her dead body under the fallen beech tree to make it look like an accident.'

'And there's another thing,' Agatha continued. 'Anthony Feldrake and Mary Carstairs said they spoke to his sister on the phone when she was in the woods. They wanted her to join them at the Feathers. She said she would, but then didn't show up and stopped answering her phone.'

Agatha slipped another couple of sheets across the desk.

'This is a list of Joan Feldrake's clothes and belongings

found on and with her body,' she said. 'Can you see what's missing?'

Toni and Patrick scanned the list. Patrick looked up with a frown and Toni's eyes were wide.

'There's no phone listed!' she said. 'What happened to her phone?'

'Either it's still there,' Patrick said, 'lost among the mud, leaves and other tree debris on the forest floor, or . . .'

'Or her murderer took it!' Agatha said. 'Perhaps to make sure no one saw the warbler message, or maybe to avoid anyone discovering something else that was on there. Either way, the missing phone is a mystery. I'm going to take a look at the scene in the woods today as soon as I've been to see Gethin Fawkes with Roy.'

As if summoned by magic, Roy Silver walked into the office.

'Did someone mention Roy Silver,' he asked, with a flourish, 'the famous author?'

He was wearing a floppy black fedora hat decorated with a pink feather, a black leather jacket over a black collarless shirt, a pink silk scarf draped round his neck, black jeans and pink Cuban-heeled boots. They stared at him in silence for a brief moment. Agatha realised that her mouth had dropped open and closed it.

'Well, that's our cover, isn't it?' Roy said defensively, looking straight at Agatha. 'I'm an author and you're helping me research . . . sheep . . .'

'You've certainly got into character,' Agatha said eventually. 'The hat and scarf are possibly too . . . theatrical . . . and those boots aren't ideal for a farm.'

'I know,' Roy said, his enthusiasm returning. 'That's why I brought these.' He produced a pair of black wellington boots decorated with pink unicorns. 'I wear them when I help out at the stables.'

'Lose the hat and scarf,' Agatha said, just as her phone began to ring, 'and grab yourself a coffee, Roy. We'll leave in ten minutes.'

With the others filing out of her office, she took the call. It was Stella Smart.

'Mrs Raisin,' said Smart, in a voice that was little more than an anxious whisper, 'I need to talk to you. It's about Joan. They *murdered* her!'

'Who murdered her, Miss Smart?' Agatha asked.

'Not now,' breathed Smart. 'The police won't believe me, but I know you can help. It's all about money and revenge! They'll be coming for me next! I need to find the evidence. I'll come to see you this afternoon.'

They agreed to meet at Agatha's office later that day and Smart rang off. Agatha sat staring into space, trying to let the fallout from this latest bombshell settle so that she could make sense of it.

'Tricky phone call?' asked Toni, standing at her office door. 'I heard the word "murdered".'

'You did,' Agatha said, and ran through the short conversation. 'Either one of our potential murder suspects is trying to throw us off the scent,' she went on, 'or this all just got a lot more complicated.'

In Tweeting Bottom, Toni parked her small hatchback outside the house belonging to one of Joan Feldrake's immediate neighbours – the house on the right. This was the one, she told herself, walking up the driveway, about whom Miss Feldrake had complained over noise and the parking of a van. All seemed quiet when she rang the doorbell and there was no sign of a van. She adjusted the spectacles sitting on her nose. She didn't actually need to wear glasses and these had plain-glass lenses but, annoyingly, they still clouded her vision slightly. When the door opened, she looked down at her clipboard to recite her introduction.

'Good morning, I'm from the university social anthropology department and we're conducting research into . . .' She paused, seeing a tall yet slightly built man in the doorway and was taken aback by his unfeasibly glossy, shoulder-length blond hair. 'Stevie Sexton?'

'You've come to the right place, baby!' the man laughed, throwing his arms wide as though accepting a round of applause.

Toni blinked, looking over her glasses at the grizzled features and wrinkled eyes that seemed far older than the hair. He hesitated when he saw her puzzled expression.

'Doesn't work, does it?' said the man, laughing and pulling off the wig to reveal close-cropped, greying hair. He hung the wig on a coat stand just inside the front door, alongside a motorcycle helmet. 'I need to go for an older Sexton look these days. I can still do the young voice but not the young look.'

'You do his voice . . .' Toni said, slowly beginning to understand. 'You impersonate Stevie Sexton?'

'I like to think of myself as a tribute act rather than an impersonator,' he said, grinning and waving her inside.

'I still make a few quid doing shows here and there in pubs and clubs. Would you like to come in?'

'I'm ... um ... not supposed to do that,' Toni said, holding up the fake ID that said she was Kate Carpenter. 'I'm really here to ask about neighbours and any problems with noise, or—'

'Oh, I had problems with noise all right,' said the man, reaching out to shake Toni's hand. 'I'm Eric Spalding. The big problem was, it was me who was making all the noise!'

'Was that because of your tribute act?' Toni asked.

'Yeah, the woman who lived next door – she died in an accident at the weekend – complained to the council about me rehearsing here. She complained about my van too. I have a market stall, so I need the van for that as well as for lugging my Stevie Sexton gear around.'

'There's no van here,' Toni said, looking round.

'I'm at the end of this row of houses,' Spalding explained, 'and there's a track down the side of the house. I keep it there, out of sight.'

'Did the council stop you rehearsing?' asked Toni.

'Nah,' the man said, grinning again. 'I soundproofed my back room, so I can sing as loud as I like now and use headphones for the backing tracks. I can show you, if you like.'

'No, thank you, Mr Spalding,' Toni declined politely. 'So you got on well with your neighbour in the end?'

'Hardly ever saw her,' Spalding said. 'Didn't much like her. She was a bit snooty, a bit stuck-up, if you know what I mean. Shame about what happened, though. Must have been dreadful.'

Toni thanked Spalding for his time and made a quick call to check in with the office before approaching Joan Feldrake's front door.

'You won't get any answer there,' came a voice from the house to her left.

Toni looked across to where a man she estimated to be in his fifties, wearing a beige cardigan and shapeless corduroy trousers, stood on his doorstep.

'I take it the owner's not at home,' Toni said.

'Joan – Miss Feldrake – passed away a few days ago,' the man informed her, 'and her brother's not there at the moment.'

'May I have a quick word with you?' Toni said, hurrying down one garden path and up the next. Standing at his doorstep, she showed her ID and explained about her research. The man introduced himself as Mr Bellingham.

'Did you get along well with Miss Feldrake?' Toni asked.

'We were very good friends,' Bellingham assured her. 'If she was ever away for any reason, Joan always dropped keys round to us so we could keep an eye on the place for her.' Then he lowered his voice and nodded towards Spalding's house. 'She never quite trusted that chap at the end. He's a strange character. A market trader. Not the sort you'd expect to live in Tweeting Bottom. He was the bane of Joan's life. She often said how lucky she felt to have us to turn to when things were bad with Spalding. She said we were her closest friends – always have been, ever since we moved in here.'

He was lying. Even if she had yet to develop anything approaching Agatha's innate sixth sense for scenting a lie, Toni knew Bellingham was not telling the truth. He and his wife had complained long and hard about Joan Feldrake's bird hide. They were certainly not her closest friends.

'Who is it, Mike?' A woman, clearly Mrs Bellingham, appeared in the hallway behind her husband. Although roughly the same age as him, she was dressed far more fashionably, with her dark hair styled in shoulder-length waves and her make-up impeccably applied. Toni introduced herself once again.

'I doubt you'll have much luck trying to get anyone else in Tweeting Bottom to talk to you,' Mrs Bellingham said. 'They all like to keep themselves to themselves. Even if they're in, some of them won't answer the door to a stranger.'

Despite Mrs Bellingham's advice, Toni continued making her way from house to house around the meadow. She had met the neighbours of most interest but still needed to make it look like she was who she said she was. At each subsequent house call she made, her conversations with the Bellinghams and Spalding were foremost in her mind and the notes she continued to make on her clipboard were all about Joan Feldrake's nearest neighbours.

Agatha and Roy drove up a rough stretch of track to Gethin Fawkes's farm with Roy at the wheel. Agatha had made a number of phone calls while they were en route, including one to Charlotte Clark, keeping her up to date. Fawkes must have seen them coming; he was standing in the farmyard where Roy drew to a halt. A black-and-white Border collie sat neatly at his feet, its ears pricked and its brown eyes fixed on the approaching vehicle.

Agatha scanned the property as they stepped out of the car. There was a small, stone-built farmhouse, its roof tiled rather than thatched like her cottage in Lilac Lane. A small barn stood close to the house, beyond which she could see another building. Fields stretched off up a hill in the distance and down to a patch of woodland where Agatha knew a river ran, although it was out of sight from where they were standing. It was in the woods down near the river that Joan Feldrake had met her fate.

Agatha introduced herself and Roy, who had brought along a notepad and pencil, trying his best to look like an author keen to learn all about life on the farm. She was pleased to see that Fawkes was wearing a battered waxed jacket over a T-shirt, jeans and wellies. It pleased her because she, too, was wearing a waxed jacket, although hers could be described more as pristine rather than battered. The weather was warm enough to go without a jacket, but it was an item of countryside uniform over which she hoped she might form some sort of bond with Fawkes. Her skirt was plain green and cotton, reaching just above her knee and loose enough for a cross-country hike.

Unlike Piper, Tamara's Labrador, Fawkes's dog had not made a move towards them. It offered neither a welcome nor a warning bark, but its eyes never left them. Fawkes took in both Agatha and Roy with a glance, his eyes settling on their feet. Neither Agatha's high heels nor Roy's luminous boots were suitable for rambling over fields.

'We have wellies in the back of the car,' Agatha said and Fawkes nodded, Agatha taking that as approval for them to change their footwear.

'I don't get many visitors – not many that I want to see, anyway,' Fawkes said, then snapped his fingers at the dog. 'Come, Molly.'

Fawkes and Molly led the way across the farmyard and up over some rough grass towards a wide metal gate. Beyond the gate was a field that climbed uphill in the sunshine, where sheep drifted lazily across the slope.

'What sort of visitors don't you want to see, Mr Fawkes?' Roy asked.

'People like you, mainly,' Fawkes said, sending a dark look from Roy to Agatha. 'People who have no business on my land.'

'Surely a few walkers don't cause you a huge problem,' Roy said.

'People tromping from one field to another, from one farm to another, can spread all sorts of diseases among livestock,' Fawkes grumbled. 'And trespassers bring dogs. Molly here is trained to work with my flock, but strangers' dogs can chase and kill sheep or even cattle. I've every right to shoot them.'

'You can shoot trespassers?' Roy said, slightly shocked.

'Sadly not,' said Fawkes. 'Just the dogs, not the trespassers.'

'We didn't come here as trespassers,' Agatha pointed out. 'We understood from Sir Charles Fraith that you would make us welcome. I thought he was your friend.'

'We're not friends,' said Fawkes. 'His sort don't make friends with the likes of me. They want us bowing and scraping to them. They don't want us as friends. In their eyes, we're beneath them and that's the way it's always been.'

'So you don't like Sir Charles?' Roy asked.

'I didn't say that,' Fawkes replied. 'He's not as bad as some of those upper-crust toffs. He's a fair man, I'll give him that. He offered me a proper price for the land he wanted to buy, even if it wasn't for sale. The bargain we made about you coming here should keep him off my back about that.'

'You know, Mr Fawkes,' Agatha said, tiring of Fawkes's attitude, 'this whole visit – your part of the bargain with Sir Charles – might go much more smoothly if you could at least try to be a bit more amenable.'

'You can have your tour,' Fawkes said, glowering at her, 'you can ask your questions, and then you can go.'

'Would it really hurt so much for you to try at least to be civil?' Agatha returned his heavy stare.

'You rich city people are a real bunch of ignorant wasters, aren't you?' he snarled. 'You come out here with all your money and buy property in the countryside, pushing prices up so high that local people on ordinary wages can't afford to buy even the smallest cottages!'

Agatha blinked, caught slightly off guard by his vehemence, then felt her back stiffen as he thundered on.

'Then you bugger off back to your posh homes in the cities, leaving your little country getaway standing empty for weeks on end while locals are struggling to find anywhere to live. You people make me sick!'

Agatha's head tilted slightly to one side. She took a deep breath and held it, feeling a surge of anger rising from somewhere down near her skirt's waistband. Who the hell did this yokel think he was, talking to her like that? He knew nothing about her! He was the ignorant one! Fawkes pushed open the gate just wide enough to get through and stepped off to the left, Molly slinking through the opening at his heels. He then let the gate's powerful spring swing it closed behind him just as Agatha stepped forward. It was the open-air version of having a door slammed in your face.

'You people don't understand one little thing about the land or our way of life,' ranted Fawkes, 'and you don't care! You're an over-privileged, selfish load of—'

'That's enough!' Agatha roared, unable to confine her rage a second longer. 'I've met a lot of nasty, spiteful, stupid people in my time, but they're all saints compared with you! You're the one who doesn't understand! You're an idiot if you think people like me don't care about the countryside! I live in Carsely – permanently – because I love it here. I run a business that employs local people and I pay them well so they can afford to live comfortably and buy their own homes if they so choose. I like the people who live around here and most are kind and intelligent. You're one of the exceptions. You're as thick and useless as a broken brick. No, I take that back – even a broken brick can hold a gate open!'

She pushed with all her might on the gate and it budged not one inch. Roy reached over and raised the latch. Agatha charged forward through the middle of the gateway and Roy stepped in to the left close to where

137

Fawkes was standing. Agatha let the gate go and it swung shut. It was only then that she realised she was standing in a patch of deep mud. She made to walk towards Fawkes and Roy but her right foot had been sucked down too deep into the mud. She couldn't shift it. She heaved on her left leg and her foot shot out of her wellie in a high kick like a country can-can dancer. Tipping slowly backwards, she began losing her balance, waving her arms desperately in circles as if trying to swim back upright. It was no good. She landed flat on her back in the mud and her dis-wellied left foot plunged beneath the surface. The feeling of the gooey mud oozing between her toes forced her to stifle a whimper.

'Gets muddy in the middle there, where there's so much coming and going,' Fawkes said. 'I suppose you'll want to be heading home now you've got a bit mucky.'

Agatha raised her head, struggling to sit up, and shot a look at him through eyes almost as narrowed as her pursed lips. She could see Molly at Fawkes's ankle and was convinced that the dog was smiling.

'I will not be going home,' Agatha stated. Her temper had evaporated somewhere around the time her dignity had sunk in the mud. Now she felt only a strange, mud-induced calm. 'I will be staying here until we've seen everything we came to see. Don't think a little bit of mud's going to put me off, Mr Fawkes!'

Roy moved forward to try to help, but Fawkes stepped in front of him. He reached out a hand to Agatha.

'I admire your pluck, Mrs Raisin,' he said.

Agatha snapped her knees together to make sure that was all he was admiring and accepted his hand.

He hauled her to her feet, then gently lifted her over to where Roy was standing on firmer ground. Both her wellies were left standing in the mud. He retrieved them for her, shaking off most of the clinging mud, and placed them on the dry ground in front of her. Molly seemed fascinated by the entire pantomime.

'The jacket's taken most of the mud, so I'll leave it here for now,' Agatha said, taking it off to hang it on the fence before scraping a hand down her backside to remove the worst of the mud clinging there. 'I'm perfectly capable of coping with the rest.'

She wiped her muddied feet with tissues supplied by Roy and accepted another to clean her hand. With her head held high, she then stepped back into her wellies.

'Lead on, Mr Fawkes,' she said. 'Let's get the tour underway.'

They walked up the hill to a vantage point where Fawkes could identify different areas of his farm.

'In all, the farm amounts to around one hundred and twenty acres. I have up to six hundred sheep on the hillside and a small herd of dairy cows in the lower pastures.' He pointed to a building a little way from the farmhouse. 'Over there is the milking parlour and the big barn is mainly used as a feed store.'

The big barn was between the milking parlour and the house, with a smaller barn to its left.

'What about that small barn near the house?' Roy asked. 'What's that used for?'

'That's private, Mr Silver,' Fawkes said. 'That's nobody's business but mine.'

As they crossed the hillside, a handful of Fawkes's sheep approached, walking straight towards him.

'Easy, Molly,' he said, and the dog lay down in the grass, monitoring every move the sheep made. The sheep ignored Agatha, Roy and the dog, nuzzling Fawkes's hand. He reached into his pocket to give them small pieces of carrot.

'That's a treat for them,' he said, smiling down at the animals. 'Most of what they need to eat is right here on the hillside. They need a bit of hay during the winter, maybe a bit of grain for the lambs, but apart from that everything they want is right here. Of all livestock, they have the healthiest life. You can't keep them indoors. They need to be outside all the time, where they're most at home.'

Agatha watched him. He seemed like a changed man when he was dealing with the animals.

'That many sheep must produce a lot of wool, Mr Fawkes,' Roy said, notebook at the ready.

'They do,' Fawkes said, 'but there's not much money in that. One of my ewes might provide four and a half kilos of wool in a year, but I'm lucky to get forty pence per kilo some years, sometimes less. At those prices it doesn't pay for the help I need to shear them all.'

'But wool is so expensive to buy,' Agatha said. 'I have a cashmere pashmina that cost me a small fortune.'

'Cashmere is goats' wool, Mrs Raisin,' Fawkes informed her, a faint smile of satisfaction crossing his face when he saw her startled expression.

'Goat?' she said.

'It is indeed,' he confirmed. 'Fine wool, as is a great

deal of lambswool. Expensive garments, but very little of the cost comes back to the farm.'

'Can't you just let their fleeces grow?' Roy asked. 'Avoid the shearing cost?'

'That would be bad for them, Mr Silver,' Fawkes explained. 'Around this time of year blowflies and the like will lay eggs in untended coats, and when the maggots hatch they start eating the animal's flesh. They have to be sheared and sprayed to keep them free of pests like that.'

'So these guys are for the meat market,' Roy said, watching one of the sheep lick Fawkes's pocket, hoping for another treat.

'Once they're grown, some of the lambs will end up as a Sunday roast dinner,' Fawkes said, nodding. 'Some I'll keep and hopefully the next season there will be more healthy lambs. I have a handful of prize rams in the field over yonder.' He pointed to a different area of hillside. 'They have to be kept separate from the ewes so I can control the whole breeding and lambing cycle.'

'That's near Jessica Barnes's place, isn't it?' Roy commented.

'Don't mention that woman around here,' Fawkes grunted. 'Those pampered pets of hers are a pain in the neck. Her walls and fences are in a terrible state and her lot are constantly finding ways through to get frisky with my rams. I put them back when I spot them and try to plug the gaps, but I've got more to do with my time than look after her little hobby flock. She's likely got some pregnant ewes in there that she doesn't even know about.'

141

'Do you work the whole farm yourself?' Agatha asked.

'There are some local lads come in to help now and again, especially around lambing time,' Fawkes said. 'I can't afford to pay for much labour. I barely make a living as it is.'

They walked down the hill, and saw the cows in their pasture and the milking parlour before Fawkes led them on a slight detour that took them past the large barn but well away from the smaller one he had deemed 'private'. They said their goodbyes at the car, whereupon Fawkes walked back towards the farmhouse where he and Molly stood to watch them drive down the track and off the property.

'I think we've probably solved the mystery of Jessica's disappearing ewes,' Agatha said, 'but I'm beginning to wonder if Gethin Fawkes had anything to do with Joan Feldrake's death.'

'I can't stop thinking about those sheep nudging their noses against his pocket,' Roy said, swinging the car onto the road towards Carsely. 'They were so sweet! I think I may have to turn vegetarian.'

'Really?' Agatha was incredulous. 'I saw the way you tucked into those sausages at Tamara's barbecue.'

'Mmmmm . . .' Roy mumbled. 'Maybe I could become a vegetarian except for sausages . . . and bacon sandwiches. I mean, who can possibly resist a bacon sandwich? Actually, I'm starting to feel quite peckish . . .'

'Just take me home, Roy,' Agatha said with a sigh. 'I need to change out of this muddy skirt so we can get down to the murder scene and take a good look around.'

'It's still a murder then?' Roy asked.

'Of course it is,' Agatha assured him. 'Gethin Fawkes remains a suspect, and we have plenty of others on the list. This is still a murder inquiry, Roy. I'd bet your next bacon sandwich on it.'

Chapter Seven

Roy sat in the sunshine in Agatha's garden, helpfully wiping the mud from her waxed jacket then fussing over the cats, while she was upstairs changing into clean clothes. She considered having the skirt professionally cleaned, then decided against it. It was binned just as the tart-stained white trousers had been.

She tried on a white summer dress with thin shoulder straps and wooden buttons down the front. Standing in front of the mirror, she was pleasantly surprised at how good it looked. She'd bought it months ago on impulse and had been worried that she didn't have the figure for this kind of dress any more, everything having developed a depressing tendency to head south. It wasn't the sort of dress with which she could wear a bra, but the bodice fitted snugly enough to hold everything in place without being too revealing. It looked cool and summery. She smiled and that brightened her look even more.

'You look sensational, darling!' Roy cooed when she appeared in the garden. 'That's not really a dress for work, though, is it?'

'We're not going to work, Roy,' she said, turning her face to the sun and holding out her arms to feel its warmth. 'We're going for a stroll in the woods and John called. He's at home today, so later this afternoon I'm meeting him to go for a walk down the riverside path beyond Mircester. The weather is so lovely I'm leaving work a little early – as soon as I've had a chat with Stella Smart.' She paused, having remembered the meeting. Thinking of John had scrambled her memory again. It wasn't like her to forget a meeting with someone so heavily involved in a murder investigation. She looked down at her bare shoulders. 'I'll wear that lovely pashmina in the office. Who'd have thought goats' wool could be so soft? John's suggested a visit to the Ferryman pub – he loves the beer there and I know I can get a decent glass of rosé.'

'Sounds delightful,' Roy said, 'but you can't go walking in the woods in those.' He pointed to the wedge-heeled sandals Agatha was wearing.

'No,' Agatha agreed, reaching inside the kitchen door to produce a pair of short, white wellies that she kept for sauntering on the lawn first thing in the morning when a little dew sometimes lingered on the grass. 'These will do for that.'

As they left the house, Agatha picked up a small, black overnight bag in the hall.

'I also had a call from Patrick,' she explained. 'He's arranged for Toni and me to talk to Boddington and Trimble early tomorrow. I'm staying with John tonight, so this is something more appropriate for a business meeting.'

'Anything for me to do tomorrow?' Roy asked as they walked out the door.

'Yes, you can talk to your friend Jessica Barnes,' Agatha said, locking the door behind them. 'Tell her she needs to do something about her walls and fences. She'd also best have a vet check out her tarty Bowmont girls to see if any of them have got themselves pregnant.'

The small lay-by on the road beside where the beech tree had fallen had no other cars, leaving plenty of space for them to park. The tree had been cut into pieces in order to clear it from the road. Some of it had obviously been removed from the scene to be disposed of elsewhere, but some had been left on the forest floor near the road to decompose and let nature take its course.

There were traces of sawdust on the road where the chainsaws had done their work. Most had been swept to the side, but some had drifted back and been spread by passing cars, the longest trails heading off towards the river, where a small stone bridge carried the road across in the direction of Ancombe. Roy scuffed at a pile of the dust with the toe of his pink boot.

'Not much chance of us finding the murder weapon,' he said.

'The police already recovered the oak branch that hit her,' Agatha said, looking up at the surrounding trees. 'That's an oak tree,' she said, pointing. 'Looks like it has some damage, so Wilkes will have convinced himself the killer branch came from there.'

Roy looked at some of the sawdust on the narrow grass verge running between the tarmac and a roadside ditch.

'Some of that stuff looks like it's bloodstained,' he said. 'Was there much blood on the road?'

'I couldn't get close enough to see,' Agatha replied. 'There must have been enough to support the accident theory, and if there was any obvious blood trail leading into the woods, Bill Wong would have spotted it. That doesn't mean Miss Feldrake wasn't attacked in the woods. The yellow anorak she was wearing and its hood could well have kept any blood trail to a bare minimum. Forget about looking for blood. What we want to find is her missing phone, if it's still here.'

The ground under the trees was covered with fallen twigs and branches, as well as thorny bramble tendrils creeping through the carpet of old leaf litter, threatening to catch your foot and trip you every few metres. Roy picked up a long stick to turn over leaves and branches, looking for the phone. Agatha trod carefully, her eyes scanning the ground right and left for anything that seemed out of place. She held her own phone in her hand.

'You know, if we had Joan Feldrake's number,' Roy said, 'we could just call her phone and listen for it ringing.'

'I do have her number, Roy,' Agatha said. 'It was in the police report, but it's coming up as unavailable.'

They walked on towards the river for a few minutes until Agatha suddenly heard her name being called. She popped her phone back into the small clutch bag she was carrying.

'Mrs Raisin,' said Mary Carstairs, stepping out from behind a tree. 'I wasn't expecting to see you here.'

'Oh, we were just passing by,' Agatha lied, 'and I wanted to take a look to . . . you know . . . settle the whole dreadful incident in my mind. What brings you here?'

'Much the same thing, really,' Carstairs replied. 'I suppose I'm looking for – what is it they call it nowadays? – some kind of closure.'

'Mr Feldrake isn't with you?' Agatha asked.

'No, he stayed at Tweeting Bottom,' Carstairs explained, pointing to her stout walking shoes, 'but I wanted to walk, get some fresh air and try to clear my head. There's so much going on, you see, with Joan's funeral on Monday at St Jude's.'

'Monday?' Agatha sounded surprised. 'Today's Wednesday. I thought these things had to be booked much further in advance.'

'Reverend Bloxby had a funeral slot free due to a cancellation,' Carstairs said.

'Really?' Agatha was amazed. 'I didn't think it was the sort of business where you had cancellations. I mean, you can't suddenly change your mind and choose to die next week rather than this week, can you?'

'Someone's family apparently decided to have the whole affair conducted by a civil celebrant at Mircester Crematorium,' Carstairs said, sniffing and looking as though she might shed another tear or two.

'I was wondering,' Agatha said slowly, choosing her next words carefully in an attempt to avoid sounding like she was interrogating Carstairs, 'why you didn't join Joan and Stella looking for the magnolia warbler? Stella said she'd had a phone message about it and that Joan must have as well. Didn't you get the message?'

'Yes, but I dismissed it as a prank,' Carstairs said. 'It wasn't from anyone that I knew or any number I recognised. Besides, I wanted to concentrate on the meeting at the Feathers.'

At that point Roy, who Agatha was fairly sure had been standing pretty still, tripped and fell headlong on the ground.

'Are you all right, Roy?' she asked.

'Yes, don't mind me,' he said with a light laugh, but making no attempt to get up. 'I'll just . . . um . . . take a moment to catch my breath.'

'Well, I must be getting back,' Carstairs said, dabbing an eye with a tissue. 'I don't want Anthony worrying about me.'

'She was lying,' Agatha said, once Carstairs was out of earshot, 'and making a far worse job of it than I did.'

'Lying about the funeral?' Roy asked, still stretched out on the ground.

'No, lying about the phone message and about why she was here,' Agatha said. 'And I didn't see any tears for her to mop up with that hankie – that was all an act. Do you think she might have been here looking for the phone, too?'

'If she was, she didn't find it,' Roy said.

'How do you know that?'

'Because I'm lying on it!'

Agatha crouched down beside him and he yanked a soil-stained phone out from beneath him. She took the phone and thumbed the power button.

'That's why it didn't ring,' Roy said, staring at the blank screen. 'It's out of charge.'

Agatha stood slowly and passed the phone back to Roy once he'd scrambled to his feet. She looked right and left, checking to see if anyone might be watching.

'I want to take a bit more of a look around,' she said, handing him her clutch bag. 'My phone's almost dead, too. There are a couple of charging cables in the central armrest of my car. The keys are in my bag. You go and start charging the phones and I'll finish off here – and be careful, Roy. You can't see far in these woods and Mary Carstairs managed to sneak up on us quite easily.'

'I'll be fine,' Roy said. 'I'll see you back at the car.'

Roy set off towards the road and Agatha continued in the direction of the river. She kept her eyes peeled for anything else that might appear on the forest floor, but as she got closer to the water, the ground underfoot became softer, the soil clearly waterlogged. When the river came in sight it was running high and fast, although it had not quite burst its banks. Rainwater from the surrounding hills was obviously still draining down into the water-way, and the speed at which floating tree debris was moving showed the strength of the current.

Following her mud bath that morning, Agatha felt decidedly unhappy about the claggy ground and was about to turn back when she thought she saw something odd in the water. She ventured a little closer and saw that it was a shoe. Closer still and she could make out a leg. When she was at the very edge of the riverbank, she leaned over to see a submerged body wedged in a jumble of reeds and tree roots.

'Snakes and bastards!' she gasped, as she found herself peering down into the cold, dead eyes of Stella Smart.

At that very moment, she felt a painful thump to her shoulders and she was falling forwards. Someone had pushed her into the water! She hit the river head-first, crashing down on top of Smart's body and tumbling over. The cold water made her gasp and she choked on a lungful, desperately pushing the corpse aside to surface momentarily, opening her eyes to catch a glimpse of a shadowy figure disappearing into the trees. Then she was dragged under again by the current and by the now dislodged body which wrapped itself around her waist.

She pushed and kicked to try to free herself from the weight of the corpse that kept dragging her under, but her boots were full of water, weighing her down even more, making her legs feel like lead. Struggling in a mad panic, she managed to fling off first one boot, then the other, and felt her face break the surface. She sucked in a huge gulp of air, using it to scream as loudly as she could.

'Roy! Help me!'

Then she was hauled under once more, the mighty force of the current moving the arms and legs of the dead body to tangle them with her own. She broke free for an instant, grabbing another quick breath of air and realising that she was now close to the far bank of the river. She was immediately swirled round and sub-merged again. Reaching one arm clear of the water, she tried to grab a low branch, a tree root or a handful of reeds – anything she could use to pull herself out of the torrent – but her fingers found only fresh air.

Then she felt something clamp around her wrist. A powerful grip stopped her chaotic charge downstream, drawing her closer to the bank. Her face was suddenly free of the water and she spluttered and coughed, heaving in as much air as she could. She felt a hand grab her free wrist and she clung on desperately, the body of Stella Smart resolutely attempting to haul her back into the river. She had her back to the bank and, when the water cleared from her eyes, she was looking out across the water. She was close to the bridge and she could see Roy sprinting across it.

'Hold on!' he panted. 'I'm coming!'

'Hurry, man!' came a deep voice from above and behind her. 'I'm losing my footing!'

The next thing she knew, Roy had flung himself flat on the bank, reaching down with one hand to grab her legs and the other to catch the collar of Stella Smart's jacket. Agatha felt herself being lifted clear of the water, hoisted up onto dry land. She saw Roy then pull Smart's body out of the river and realised that she was lying on someone's legs. She looked up into the face of Gethin Fawkes.

'Twice in one day, Mrs Raisin.' He grinned, panting for breath. 'Twice today I've lifted you out of a mess. It's becoming a habit.'

'Thank you,' she croaked, coughing, gulping down air and pushing her wet hair out of her eyes.

'Umm . . .' he said, looking down at her dress. 'You might want to . . .'

During the struggle in the water, the buttons down the front of her dress had come undone, revealing far more than was ever intended. She pulled it closed and sat up. Fawkes stood and took two paces to where Roy sat, breathing hard.

152

'Too late for this one,' Roy said, his chest heaving. 'She's gone.'

'Reckon you're right,' Fawkes said, taking off his jacket to cover Smart's face.

'Wait!' Agatha said, shuffling over to them, dripping water everywhere. 'I want to see her.'

Her dress fell open again and both men looked away. She moved Fawkes's jacket aside, and examined the corpse.

'You've got a bit of strength in those city-boy arms, Mr Silver,' Fawkes said, holding out a hand to shake with Roy. 'Not sure I could have got her out without you.'

'She's a very dear friend,' Roy said. 'I can't thank you enough for saving her. It was lucky you were around. What were you doing down here?'

'The woods on both sides of this stretch of river are on my land,' Fawkes said. 'What were *you* doing down here?'

'Trespassing, obviously,' Agatha said, standing in front of them with her arms folded across her chest. 'I've got the dress closed but now it's drenched it's gone transparent. We're going to have to wait here for the police, but I'm not standing around like this. Roy, would you please fetch the car? My overnight bag has everything I need in it to make myself decent, even a small towel and a pair of shoes. Mr Fawkes, can I ask you to call the police and tell them there's been a murder and an attempted murder?'

Fawkes pulled a phone from his back pocket and walked up towards the road, looking for better reception. Roy turned towards the bridge, but Agatha stopped him.

153

'Take this,' she whispered, unfolding her arms where she had hidden yet another phone. 'Stella Smart's. Took it from her pocket. Could be useful.'

Agatha borrowed Fawkes's phone to call John. She displayed no hysterics and shed no tears. She simply told him that someone had tried to kill her. He yelled in alarm that he'd be there straight away and, in fact, beat the first police car to the scene. By the time his car screeched to a halt at the side of the road, Agatha had dried herself off, ordered Roy and Fawkes to look away while she dressed in fresh clothes and even repaired her make-up, although there was little she could do about her bedraggled hair.

'Are you all right?' John asked, hugging her tight and looking down at Smart's body, the upper half covered by Fawkes's jacket. 'What the hell happened here?'

Agatha took John aside and, leaning against his car while Roy and Fawkes chatted by the river, she told him all about finding the phone and being shoved into the water. It was then that she started to feel overwhelmed by it all and stifled a sob. He held her in his arms.

'Oh, bugger!' she groaned, spotting the first police vehicles arriving and a familiar figure disembarking from an unmarked car. 'It's Wilkes. He's going to want to take me in for an interview.'

'That really shouldn't be necessary—' John began.

'He'll do it anyway,' Agatha interrupted him, opening her purse and shoving a ten-pound note into John's hand. 'Here, take this. I've just paid you. You work for me now.'

Looking slightly confused, John shoved the note into his trouser pocket as Wilkes approached.

'Well, well, if it isn't Agatha Raisin,' the DCI said, sneering. 'In trouble yet again.'

'Agatha is a victim here, not—' John said angrily, but Agatha put a hand on his arm to calm him.

'I'm not in any trouble. I've done nothing wrong,' Agatha said. It wasn't entirely true. She had appropriated evidence in the shape of Joan Feldrake's phone and had stolen Stella Smart's phone. 'You, on the other hand, Wilkes, could find yourself in big trouble over this.'

'Me?' Wilkes said, laughing. 'I think you're delusional, Mrs Raisin. Did you have a bump on the head when you went for a dip?' He took a good look at her head, glanced at her eyes and took a step back to assess the way she was standing. 'No – no signs of any injury. I think you're in good condition to be taken in for an interview.'

'I've been in the river, Wilkes,' Agatha said slowly, keeping her temper under control. 'It all looked a bit mucky in there. I've dried off, but I'm not clean. Who knows what sort of bugs or infections I might have picked up? Do you really want to sit in an interview room with me before I've had a chance to get cleaned up?'

'Well, I . . .' Wilkes eyed her suspiciously, taking a couple of steps further away to distance himself from any potential airborne infection.

'Why don't I take Mrs Raisin home, sir?' Bill Wong had arrived and joined them, having caught the tail end of the conversation. 'She lives close by, on the way to Mircester. I can wait while she sorts herself out and then bring her in.'

'See to it, Sergeant Wong,' Wilkes said, turning to walk

away, 'and I want the weirdo with the pink boots and the farmer as well.'

'John's coming, too,' Agatha said.

'Did you see any of what happened here?' Wilkes asked, turning to John.

'No, but—' John began.

'Glass won't be required,' Wilkes said, pausing to look back over his shoulder. 'He didn't witness anything.'

'I happen to know that my solicitor is on holiday right now,' Agatha said, 'so I have retained Mr Glass, with his knowledge and experience of police matters, as my legal adviser.'

Wilkes stared at her, then at John, who nodded.

'Whatever . . .' Wilkes said, waving a dismissive hand and walking away, tutting to himself.

'Sorry, Agatha,' Bill said. 'He's going to try to come down hard on you.'

'I'm not scared of Wilkes,' Agatha said with a thin smile, looking like she was enjoying the prospect of going up against her nemesis. 'All I need is a shower and I'll be ready for him.'

John watched uniformed officers stringing blue-and-white police tape between the bridge and the trees, sealing off the area by the riverbank where Stella Smart's body still lay.

'Best get them to cordon off the woods on the other side of the river, Bill,' he said, pointing. 'Agatha and Roy went from the lay-by to the gap in the trees upstream over there. That's where the body was in the water and where Agatha was attacked.'

Bill nodded and relayed the instructions, leaving

two other detectives in charge of the body before he, Agatha and John drove in convoy to Lilac Lane. John and Bill waited outside while Agatha went in to wash and change, carrying her overnight bag. Instead of going upstairs, however, she walked straight through to her kitchen, opened her bag and pulled out both Joan Feldrake's and Stella Smart's phones, which Roy had left in her car. She wrapped them in a tea towel, grabbed some keys from a drawer and made her way out into the back garden. Precisely five paces along the high hedge that divided her garden from James's, she came to a patch where she knew she could push her way through. She then used the spare keys James had given her to let herself in through his back door unseen. James had left for Iceland, but all she needed to do was leave the two phones in a kitchen drawer, where they would be safe should Wilkes decide to search her home. She then made her way back to her own cottage and upstairs for a hugely refreshing shower.

Agatha and John were ushered into an interview room once Bill had chauffeured them to Mircester Police Station. They were then kept waiting for what seemed like an eternity. John became more and more irritated as time went by but Agatha remained calm, nursing her wrath. Wilkes had left her in limbo like this many times previously and it gave her all the time she needed to consider the questions he might ask and how best to answer them. He would, doubtless, expect her to lose her temper and she was pretty sure she wasn't going to disappoint him. They sat in the room for more than two hours before Wilkes strode in with Bill Wong at his shoulder.

'I hope you've been offered tea or coffee,' Wilkes said, dropping a file on the table and sitting opposite Agatha and John. 'We like to make our prisoners as comfortable as we can.'

'We are not your prisoners,' Agatha pointed out, frowning at Wilkes. She'd imagined all sorts of things he might say, but that hadn't been one of them. 'We haven't been arrested or otherwise detained. We are here voluntarily to help you with your inquiries.'

'Did you tell her to say that?' Wilkes said, looking at John and cocking his head towards Agatha.

'You don't seem to understand who you have here,' John said, sitting back and folding his arms. 'This is Agatha Raisin. It would take a far braver man than me to tell her what she can and can't say.'

'Well, she can say a few things to me,' Wilkes sneered. 'You can start by telling me why you went down to the woods today – if you say anything about a teddy bears' picnic, I'll—'

'We were in the woods doing your job,' Agatha said bluntly. 'We were investigating the murder of Joan Feldrake.'

'I don't need you doing my job!' Wilkes snapped. 'An amateur like you has no chance of investigating a crime to the professional level of a senior police officer like myself!'

'You're right!' Agatha snapped back. 'To reach your level I'd have to drop my own standards through the floor!'

'Let's just calm down a bit, shall we?' John said, holding out his hands as though patting out a fire. 'Sniping at each other won't get us anywhere.'

'I agree,' Bill said. 'It will only make things worse.'

'Very well.' Wilkes nodded, pressing his fingertips on the table, making his skinny hands look like two giant, five-legged spiders. 'How did you come to end up in the river?'

Agatha explained how she had spotted something in the water and, when she had gone to take a closer look, someone had sneaked up behind her and pushed her in. She missed out the minor details about Feldrake and Smart's phones. She was absolutely sure that Roy, had Wilkes already spoken to him, would have done the same.

'That all sounds very . . . well rehearsed, Mrs Raisin,' Wilkes said with a sigh, 'but it doesn't help with our little problem.'

'Problem?' Agatha asked. 'What problem?'

'The problem I have with you, Mrs Raisin,' Wilkes said.

'Is that so?' Agatha said, leaning forward, her elbows on the table. 'Well, you can solve any problem you have with me by writing it down on a piece of paper, folding it, putting it in an envelope and shoving it up your—'

'Agatha, that's really not very helpful,' John said quietly.

'I've tried being helpful,' she replied. 'I've tried to help by going after the truth – by not dismissing Joan Feldrake's death as some sort of accident.'

'And it looks very much like you were right about

that,' John agreed. 'In light of what's happened today, that case will have to be reopened.'

'I am the one who decides when cases are reopened!' Wilkes barked. 'I decide whether there's been a murder or not, and right now, I'm inclined to believe there has been. You see, Mrs Raisin, the story about Mr Silver going to charge your phone and you then being attacked just doesn't ring true. Neither Mr Silver nor Mr Fawkes saw anyone near the riverbank with you. Neither of them saw you being pushed in. It seems all they saw was you fighting in the water with Stella Smart – and Miss Smart ended up dead.'

'She was already dead when I was pushed in on top of her!' Agatha objected.

'We've only your word for that,' Wilkes said. 'I believe you had an altercation with Miss Smart on the riverbank and that, during the struggle, you both fell in. You continued to fight in the water and you held her under. You murdered Stella Smart.'

'That's utter bollocks!' Agatha roared. 'I'm a victim here, not a criminal!'

'That remains to be seen!' Wilkes yelled, standing and picking up his paperwork. 'I'm now required elsewhere but, Sergeant Wong, I want this one,' he pointed to Agatha, 'formally arrested on suspicion of murder and this one,' he pointed at John, 'arrested as an accessory. I don't think they're at risk of absconding, so you can then release them under investigation, but seize their passports nevertheless.'

He made for the door but John jumped in front of him.

'You can't do this, Wilkes!' he shouted, red-faced with

anger. Agatha stood and put her hand on John's shoulder.

'Let it go, John,' she said. 'The sooner we're out of here, the sooner we can start proving our innocence.'

Wilkes stalked out of the room, leaving Agatha and John to sit down again opposite Bill.

'I'm so sorry, Agatha,' Bill said. 'And for you, John, but—'

'Just get on with it, Bill,' Agatha said, and sat back to listen to her rights being recited.

When they eventually walked free from the station, it was early evening, and as soon as they hit the fresh air, Agatha realised she had eaten nothing since the toast and coffee she'd had for breakfast.

'It's not every day you get arrested for murder,' she said. 'I think that calls for a celebration! We should be able to get a table at the Italian restaurant near my office. Fancy some pasta?'

'Sounds good to me,' John replied and offered his arm as they strolled off towards the high street. After a few seconds, Agatha stopped in her tracks.

'John!' she said. 'They're confiscating our passports! If you don't get yours back smartish you won't be able to join the cruise!'

'I know,' he replied, 'but that doesn't matter now. I'd already decided I wasn't going. There will be other cruises, but you don't seriously think I could leave you here when someone has just tried to kill you, do you? We need to find out who's behind this. I'm not going on any cruise right now.'

161

'You're doing that for me?' she said.

'Of course,' he said, smiling and taking her in his arms. 'I'd do anything for you.'

She kissed him and after a moment he pulled away, looking up and down the street.

'Now that felt very much like the sort of display of public affection that . . .' he said, an eyebrow raised in mock surprise before she told him to shut up and kissed him again.

'Come on,' she said, taking his hand and marching off towards the restaurant. 'I'm famished and we've got a long list of murder suspects to discuss!'

The restaurant had tables to spare, and the waiter offered them one in a quiet corner where they could chat without being overheard. Their first discussion was about food, Agatha eventually settling for seafood linguine loaded with fresh shrimp, clams and mussels. John chose a creamy spaghetti carbonara liberally laced with pancetta, and they opted to share a bottle of Gavi. Just as the wine was delivered to their table, Agatha's phone rang. It was Charlotte Clark.

'I hear you've found yourself in a spot of bother,' she said. 'Another murder, with you in the frame.'

'It's true, Charlotte,' Agatha said, 'but if you can keep my name out of it for a day or so while I sort a few things out, I'll give you the full story, straight from the horse's mouth.'

Charlotte readily agreed, and they rang off.

'Trying to stay out of the limelight?' John asked.

'Toni and I have a meeting tomorrow morning with Boddington's, the accountancy firm that Smart took over. It might be better if they didn't know I've been accused of her murder.'

By the time their food had been served and polished off, they had discussed the events of the day and were considering their cast of suspects.

'First on the list has to be Gethin Fawkes,' John said as Agatha ordered coffee. 'You heard him threaten all three of the twitchers and both Joan Feldrake and Stella Smart were killed on his property.'

'True,' Agatha said, 'and he was at the scene when Stella Smart died, but he pulled me out of the water. Why would he do that? And it couldn't have been him who shoved me in, because he wouldn't have been able to get down to the bridge to reach the spot where he dragged me out without Roy spotting him.'

'He could have an accomplice,' John pointed out. 'Remember, Smart told you on the phone that "they" would be coming for her next. If he's working with someone else, that unknown person could have murdered Smart and pushed you into the water in order to get away without being seen.'

'That still doesn't explain why Fawkes chose to put himself in the picture by rescuing me,' Agatha reasoned. 'There is something strange about that little barn on his farm, though. Everyone thinks something's going on there. Does that something involve a mystery accomplice? I suppose Fawkes has to remain a suspect, even if he did save my life.'

'Surely Stella Smart was also a suspect in the murder

of Joan Feldrake,' said John. 'I guess that now she's been killed as well, we can rule her out.'

'Not necessarily,' Agatha contradicted him. 'Smart was at the scene of Feldrake's death. The three friends were constantly falling out. Maybe Feldrake annoyed Smart just too much, one final time. Smart flew into a fury and whacked Feldrake in the woods, then dumped her body under the tree to make it look like an accident. Smart's phone call to me could have been to throw us off the scent. She might then have been murdered by someone else in revenge for Feldrake's death.'

'Who would want revenge?' John asked, pausing as the waiter delivered their coffees and complimentary glasses of limoncello. 'I think that idea brings us to Mary Carstairs. She and Anthony Feldrake have a longstanding grudge against Joan Feldrake and Stella Smart for scuppering their relationship all those years ago. They were at the scene when Joan Feldrake died, and you saw Carstairs at the scene of Stella Smart's murder. They're also moving with indecent haste to get rid of Joan's belongings and get her buried.'

'I agree that's weird,' Agatha nodded, then tried the sweet, lemony liqueur. Smacking her lips in satisfaction, she went on. 'Yet they could simply be anxious to get on with their lives, and we mustn't forget that Gethin Fawkes threatened all three twitchers. He might not be the only person they've fallen out with. Mary Carstairs may be frightened that she's about to become the murderer's next victim. Nevertheless, they have motive, opportunity and they've lied to us – that puts them pretty high up the suspect list.

'Then we have Boddington and Trimble from the accountants. They certainly have cause to hate Stella Smart and Joan Feldrake, but they're an unknown quantity at the moment. We'll know more about them once Toni and I have talked to them tomorrow morning.'

'And there are Joan Feldrake's neighbours,' John said. 'She'd complained about them, and they'd complained about her. Clearly they weren't on good terms.'

'The trouble with her neighbours sounds like minor stuff,' Agatha said, 'but minor problems in a quiet little place like Tweeting Bottom, where people have little else to think about, can easily escalate into major problems that take over your life. No matter how big those problems got, though, why would any of Feldrake's neighbours want to murder Stella Smart? What's the connection there? Again, I'll know more about the neighbours when I hear from Toni tomorrow at our catch-up meeting.'

'I'd like to come along to that meeting,' John said, grinning and waving the ten-pound note he'd pulled out of his pocket. 'After all, I'm on the payroll now!'

'That would be great,' Agatha said. 'I'm pulling Simon out of the mall for a day or so in case his targets start to get suspicious of him being there too often. Toni and I are meeting Bellingham and Trimble first thing, so the catch-up will be at eleven thirty.'

'I'll be there,' John said.

'In the meantime,' Agatha said, waggling her eyebrows to tempt him, 'I have Joan Feldrake's and Stella Smart's phones. Why don't we take a cab back to my place and have a look at them?'

'I'd love to,' John said, sounding weary, 'but this lovely meal and all of today's excitement have left me feeling totally knackered. I also have to compose a delicate email to the cruise line telling them that I've been wrongly arrested and can't leave the country until I've cleared my name – and yours. I think I need to head home.'

Agatha frowned for just a moment, disappointed that John didn't share her excitement about trawling through data on the murdered women's phones, then smiled when she saw him looking worried. He'd been a police detective all his life. He'd spent years reviewing evidence day after day to build cases against suspects. Why should he be excited about spending half the night staring at phone screens that probably wouldn't tell them anything they didn't already know?

'You do look a bit tired,' she said gently. 'Get some rest. I'll need you on top of your game tomorrow morning!'

As soon as she got home, Agatha headed for the kitchen, fed the cats, who were complaining loudly about having been neglected for so long, then sneaked round to James's cottage to collect the phones.

Feldrake's phone had not fully charged in the short time it had been in her car, so she plugged it in in her kitchen, then, the night warm and still, she sat in a garden chair at a small table on the patio at her back door. She congratulated herself on having bought wooden garden chairs with comfortable cushions and on having made herself an excellent gin and tonic, a drink she considered refreshingly suitable for any time of day providing the weather was warm.

Smart's phone was housed in a leather case along with a couple of bank cards, a credit card and her driving licence. Agatha tutted. Everything required for identity theft, all in one place. Had Smart ever lost her phone while she was alive, she might well have ended up losing a whole lot more. The modern credit-card-sized driving licence even gave her address, her date of birth and a fair representation of her signature. She used the tea towel in which she had wrapped the phones to wipe some dribbles of water from Smart's device, then pressed the button to start it. The phone was relatively new and waterproof. It lit up straight away, but required a pin code to access it.

Agatha took a look at Smart's driving licence, shook her head at the unflattering photo, then tried different combinations of Smart's date of birth as the pin. The third attempt worked a treat.

What she then saw in the message archive almost made her choke on her gin and tonic.

Chapter Eight

The garden was in complete darkness beyond the patches of light falling through the open back door and the kitchen window. Agatha stiffened when she heard a rustling sound and felt, rather than saw, a wisp of movement in the blackness at the bottom of the hedge. She peered at the spot and eventually made out the shadowy shapes of Boswell and Hodge, hunting bugs and other small creatures with what her blundering pets considered to be the utmost stealth. She returned to Stella Smart's screen.

Having scrolled through Smart's messages, she had come across one from the day of the murder, the message that had lured Smart to the woods where Joan Feldrake had died.

MAGNOLIA WARBLER. ANCOMBE VALE.

The message hadn't come from anyone on Smart's contacts list, but from an anonymous number. It was a message sent on Friday, however, the day before the murder, that had shocked Agatha. The number of the sender had been withheld and the message read:

> You have ruined our lives! No more! We've had enough!
> You're going to get what's coming to you!

That was a clear threat. Stella Smart had been threatened on the day the three twitchers gave their talk to Carsely Ladies Society. She hadn't seemed too concerned on the evening of the talk, even when Gethin Fawkes had burst in. Maybe she hadn't taken the message seriously then, but when Agatha had seen her by the fallen tree the following day, she had been truly shaken. Who had sent the message? Could it have been the murderer? Why threaten Stella Smart and then kill Joan Feldrake? Maybe Joan had been threatened, too! Agatha rushed into the kitchen to fetch Feldrake's phone. It had charged enough. She switched it on.

Sitting back down, she took a swig of her drink. She needed a pin code to access Feldrake's phone, just as she had done with Smart's. Fortunately, she knew Feldrake's birth date from the reports Bill had handed to her and John. The same format of date numbers that Stella Smart had used also worked with Feldrake's phone. Agatha went straight to the messages, immediately finding the one about the magnolia warbler. She noted that it had been sent well before the identical message to Stella Smart. There was, however, no hint of a death threat and, having spent the remainder of her gin and tonic trawling through them, no other messages of any apparent interest until she came across one to Smart.

> We have to stop him! He's desecrating the SS legacy!
> He's a fiend and we need to get rid of him!

Quite who the fiend was, Agatha couldn't tell, but Smart's reply to Feldrake was equally alarming.

Don't worry. He won't be around much longer.
His days are numbered.

Clearly the two women were plotting against someone. Could that be why they were murdered? Was Mary Carstairs also involved? If these messages were about the murderer, then Carstairs was certainly in danger of becoming the next victim! She had not been included, however, on the list of recipients in this exchange of messages.

Agatha checked back on Smart's phone, but the message had clearly been deleted and there were no recent messages to Mary Carstairs. Maybe Smart had been a bit more circumspect than Feldrake when it came to keeping potentially incriminating material on her phone.

She opened the photo gallery on Feldrake's phone and scrolled through countless, mostly fairly pleasant, images of the Cotswold countryside and hundreds of pictures of birds of all shapes and sizes. That was what Agatha had expected to see. One thing that surprised her was that, unlike any other suspect's or victim's phone photo collections she had examined, there were no people in the pictures. There were no family shots, no shots of friends, no humans at all, as Agatha skipped rapidly through pages of tightly packed images. Then she thought she saw a face, or at least something that looked like flesh, and she opened the photo to view it full screen. There was certainly a face and, indeed, rather a lot of flesh. In fact, to her astonishment, there was a whole series of images featuring two men and a woman engaging in what appeared to be consensual sexual activity.

None of the subjects appeared to be professional models posing for the photos. They were laughing, holding drinks and generally looked like they were enjoying themselves. Agatha didn't recognise any of them but, turning the phone this way and that, the setting looked oddly familiar. They were outdoors, but only just. They were outside a house with French windows that opened on to a patio where they were cavorting on sunloungers. The photos had been taken from a distance and she could see plants that were in bloom and others in full leaf, so it was clearly summer. It would have to be, she presumed, to get up to that sort of thing outdoors. In a couple of the photos there was what seemed like part of a tree in the immediate foreground at the edge of the image. The pictures looked for all the world like the kind of photos Agatha could only dream of getting when working a divorce case – positive proof of an illicit sexual encounter. Yet these photos went way beyond anything Agatha or her team had ever taken.

Deciding she'd seen enough, she closed the phone, locked up the house and headed for bed, pausing at the foot of the stairs to laugh to herself. Tomorrow's catch-up meeting was certainly going to be entertaining!

The following morning, Agatha and Toni met in Mircester High Street close to a modern office block that was home to Boddington's, the accountancy firm.

The building housed several different companies and they were buzzed through the main entrance when they pressed the button marked 'Boddington's' and identified themselves. They then took the lift to the first floor, where they were greeted by a receptionist who left her desk to lead them through to the main, open-plan office space.

A dozen staff sat in front of computer screens at desks that were arranged in three blocks. The bland office space had windows on three walls which provided uninspiring views of the drab architecture in Mircester's concrete city centre. This area lacked any of the characterful old buildings that filled the streets around the Raisin Investigations office, even though it was only a few minutes' walk away. The enthusiasm of architects and town planners in the 1960s and '70s for tearing down centuries-old buildings and replacing them with dreary, grey concrete had not endured among the general populace into the twenty-first century. The people of Mircester, however, were stuck with the town centre that the powers that be had bequeathed them, whether they liked it or not.

The receptionist led them into a large meeting room separated from the main office by a glass wall. She offered them coffee and Agatha and Toni seated themselves at a long boardroom table. Alan Trimble was first to join them. Agatha studied him as he introduced himself. He was a thin man with a thin, grey face and thin, black hair. He wore spectacles with heavy black frames that looked like they pulled his face forward, seemingly causing his slightly stooped stance. He was followed into the room by a woman in her late forties with short, curly blonde hair. Like Mr Trimble, she carried a notepad and pen, but she also had a buff folder under her arm.

'Good morning,' she said. 'I'm Jane Boddington.'

Agatha introduced herself and Toni, then said: 'We were expecting to meet with Keith Boddington.'

'Keith's my husband,' said Mrs Boddington. 'Unfortunately, he is unwell.'

'I'm sorry to hear that,' Agatha said. 'I do hope it's nothing serious.'

'Back trouble and exhaustion,' Mrs Boddington said, shaking her head, 'caused by the stress he's been under over the past few months.'

'Have we come at a bad time?' Toni asked, then launched into their cover story. 'It's just that our regular accountant is about to retire and we need to find someone to handle Raisin Investigations' payroll and tax affairs.'

'We may be busy, Miss Gilmour,' said Mr Trimble, 'but we won't turn away new business. Can I ask how you heard about us?'

'I recently met Joan Feldrake,' Agatha said. 'Sadly, she died in an accident the other day, but I believe she used to work here.'

'Joan Feldrake . . .' Mrs Boddington drummed on her notepad with her pen. 'She did work here. She's the reason I've had to come back to work. I had retired from the firm, but now I'm right back in the harness. I hate to speak ill of the dead, Mrs Raisin, but Joan Feldrake and Stella Smart have ruined our lives. Now, at least, we have a chance to get back on track.'

Mrs Boddington took a copy of that morning's *Mircester Telegraph* from the buff folder and showed the front-page headline about the murder of Stella Smart.

'Yes, I know about that,' Agatha said. 'Terrible business. It must have been a shock for you to read about it in the *Telegraph*.'

'It was, but that's also how we heard about Joan Feldrake,' Mrs Boddington said. 'We've hardly left the office for weeks.'

'We've been working like dogs for Stella Smart,' said Mr Trimble. 'Keith, Jane and I were in the office when Joan Feldrake died on Saturday, and we were here yesterday, of course, when Stella Smart died. That will change everything. Now we can properly look to the future.'

'How do their deaths make such a difference to you?' Toni asked.

Mrs Boddington looked uncertainly towards Mr Trimble, who simply shrugged.

'It's no real secret,' he said, 'especially now – and it's nothing a detective like Mrs Raisin couldn't easily find out for herself. Stella Smart was the company's major shareholder. She was able to award herself all sorts of bonuses and basically force us to run the company purely for her benefit. When we originally issued shares, it was to fund expansion of the business, but she put a stop to that for her own short-term gain. Now we're in a position to forge ahead again.'

'How does Miss Smart's death help you to "forge ahead"?' Agatha asked, impressed by the fresh flush of enthusiasm in Mr Trimble's previously morose expression.

174

'Stella Smart's will,' said Mrs Boddington. 'She had no close family and left pretty much everything to Joan Feldrake and Mary Carstairs. When it came to her shares in the company, however, they were to come to the Boddington's company directors – my husband, myself and Mr Trimble.'

'She used that will like a bullwhip,' Mr Trimble said, surprising both Agatha and Toni by demonstrating a whip-cracking motion with his arm. 'She used it to keep us in line. She'd be making horrendous demands one minute and the next she'd be reminding us that in her will, the company would be returned to us one day – but only if we did as she said. The threat was always that she would change the will, leaving us high and dry.'

'She did the same with her friends,' said Mrs Boddington. 'Always threatening to cut them out of her will. Now, however, we're free of her and busy preparing for the future.'

'So, as soon as you're ready to talk specifics,' said Mr Trimble, 'we're ready to do business.'

Agatha and Toni left Boddington's shortly afterwards, having explained a little about Raisin Investigations to maintain their subterfuge. As soon as the lift doors closed, Toni turned to Agatha.

'Well, that was . . .' Toni started to say, then caught the look in Agatha's eye and took in the almost imperceptible shake of her head, prompting her to change tack, '. . . most informative. They seemed like jolly nice people.'

Once they were out in the street, walking towards their own office, Agatha explained.

'They can't be trusted,' she said. 'I wouldn't put it past them to have bugged the lift. There was definitely a security camera in there.'

'They certainly had plenty to gain from Miss Smart's murder,' Toni said.

'They did,' Agatha agreed, running through the meeting in her head, 'and there was something about what Jane Boddington said ... Come on, Toni, let's get back and talk all this through.'

When they walked into Raisin Investigations, the office boasted a full complement of staff. Patrick and Simon were working at their desks, as was Mrs Freedman, while Roy and John were sitting at a spare desk chatting.

'Right, everyone!' Agatha said, calling her team to attention and handing two phones to Simon. 'I've got a lot to share with you and I need you all focused. Simon, I will need these phones hooked up to a bigger screen so we can all see them when we're ready. Helen, I'm going to need—' She stopped herself as Mrs Freedman appeared at her elbow with the coffee for which she had just been about to ask. She nodded her thanks and took a sip.

'Agatha, darling, are you all right?' Roy came towards her, looking hugely concerned.

Roy and John had clearly told everyone else about the previous day's excitement on the riverbank and subsequent events, but Toni had missed the debrief. She looked at Agatha, mystified.

'Ah, yes ...' Agatha said slowly, giving Toni an

apologetic smile. 'Someone tried to kill me yesterday and I got arrested for murder. Forgot to mention it.'

'Forgot to . . .?' Toni stomped over to her desk and parked the small briefcase she had been carrying, muttering, 'Bloody hell . . .'

Agatha went into her own office, dropped her handbag into its drawer, then dragged her spare chair out into the main office, sitting beside Toni's desk. For Toni's benefit, Agatha gave a quick recap on her ordeal the previous day.

'Agatha, when I gave my statement, I said nothing about you "fighting" in the water with Miss Smart,' Roy said. 'I'm pretty sure Gethin wouldn't have said that either. I think he rather admires you.'

'Sounds like Wilkes playing games,' John said. 'He'll have taken anything you or Fawkes might have said about "struggling" or "grappling" and seen that as fighting.'

'Be that as it may,' Agatha said, 'I'm now his prime suspect, which means he'll be looking for ways to prove me guilty rather than looking for the real killer, which is now our top priority.'

'"Gethin"?' Simon said, raising an eyebrow towards Roy. 'Your new best friend?'

'I helped him save Agatha,' Roy said defensively. 'You might say we're brothers in arms.'

'Let's get on now,' Agatha said, silencing any chat. 'Simon, we'll start with you before we move on to the murders. What's the state of play with the shoplifters?'

'I was writing up a report as you arrived, Boss,' Simon said. 'I tailed a couple of the thieves yesterday and, as expected, they led me all the way down to the old cathedral walls. I made sure I stayed out of sight, but I managed to use that gizmo you gave me – the monocular – with my phone to get a few photos.'

He turned his computer screen round so that everyone could see the photos displayed clearly at a decent size.

'The guy who took the goods – mainly expensive aftershaves – from the thieves is the same one I've seen there before. He paid them in wraps of some kind of drugs. You can see his face quite clearly in this picture, but I've no idea who he is.'

'I do,' Toni said, standing to step forward and take a closer look at the screen. 'No doubt about it – that's Stevie Sexton! I mean, Eric Spalding. He's one of Joan Feldrake's neighbours. He does a Sexton tribute act in pubs and clubs. He also has a market stall.'

'A perfect set-up,' Patrick said. 'He's trading drugs for goods that he can sell on his stall.'

'It's clever,' John said, nodding his head in agreement, 'but he's only dishing out piddling amounts to his shoplifters. He'll be able to distribute far bigger quantities of drugs in pubs and clubs, and when he takes his stall to the various markets across the region.'

'Excellent! Good work, Simon, and you, Toni,' Agatha said. 'Get whatever details Toni can give you on Spalding, Simon, then we can give the mall management our findings and hand the whole lot over to Bill Wong. Now, let's move on to the murders . . .'

She outlined the list of suspects just as she and John had discussed them in the restaurant the previous evening, then asked for Simon to display elements from Stella Smart's phone on his screen.

'This morning, we learned that Stella Smart's shares

in Boddington's will go to the three company directors – Keith Boddington, Jane Boddington and Alan Trimble. Boddington's will become a family firm once again,' Agatha explained.

'So not only did they have cause to hate Miss Smart and Miss Feldrake,' Toni took up the story, 'but they also stood to benefit from Miss Smart's death.'

'And there's another thing,' Agatha added. 'Remember what Jane Boddington said this morning, Toni? She said that Feldrake and Smart "have ruined our lives". Simon, can you pull up a text message from last Friday? It has the number withheld.'

On screen appeared the message:

> You have ruined our lives! No more! We've had
> enough! You're going to get what's coming to you!

'Same phrase,' Simon said, staring at the screen, '"ruined our lives". Quite a coincidence.'

'And what do we say about coincidences, Simon?' Agatha asked.

'No such thing as a coincidence in a murder investigation, Boss,' Simon answered, reciting one of Agatha's mantras with a wide grin.

'Alan Trimble claims that he and the Boddingtons have alibis for the murders – that they were in the office,' Agatha said. 'See if you can find a way to check those alibis, Simon. I'm sure that threat came from Jane Boddington. Making a threat doesn't make her a murderer, but it's a mark against them nonetheless.

'Now, the following day, the day of Feldrake's murder, there's a message about the magnolia warbler in

Ancombe Vale,' Agatha said, pausing while Simon displayed the message. 'I think this message came from a different source than the threat – the number's not withheld, it's from an unknown phone. The same message is on Joan Feldrake's phone, from the same number, but was sent more than two hours earlier.'

'If that had been an alert from a birdwatching group,' Patrick said, 'it would have gone out to a whole address list of anyone who might be interested, all at the same time.'

'But it didn't,' Agatha said. 'As far as we know, it didn't go out to anyone else. No other birdwatchers turned up.'

'Mary Carstairs claims to have received that message,' Roy pointed out, 'but chose to ignore it.'

'True,' Agatha said, 'but we've only her word that she received the message, and I don't think she's been telling us the whole truth. She may have been another potential victim, but she remains a suspect.'

'If the message was sent to lure Feldrake, Smart and Carstairs to the site,' John said, 'the intention might have been to deal with them one at a time.'

'Or maybe to murder Feldrake and Carstairs, then have Smart find the bodies,' Patrick said. 'They could have planned to frame Smart for the murders.'

'Good thinking,' Agatha said. 'So whether it was a multiple murder or a frame-up, what stopped them?'

'The tree!' Roy said, standing in the middle of the gathering and swishing his arms in the air like branches in a wind. 'When it came crashing down' – he leaned over as far as he dared without crashing down himself

– 'it would have made a horrendous noise. Only a matter of time before someone came to check that out and, of course, it fell across the road. That's a quiet road, but a few cars were bound to get snarled up there eventually.'

'Sounds plausible,' said John. 'They had to make their getaway, so they dumped the body under the tree and legged it.'

'Any of our suspects would have made their getaway at that point,' Agatha said, 'except Anthony Feldrake and Mary Carstairs. They were still there when we arrived.'

'So was Stella Smart,' Simon pointed out.

'Yes, but I'm not convinced by the theory that Smart killed Feldrake and was later murdered in the same spot,' Agatha said, concentrating hard on searching her memory. 'I think the same murderers killed them both but there's something about the murder scene that doesn't ring true and I can't quite put my finger on it. Simon, can we take a look at the other phone, please?'

Simon displayed material from Joan Feldrake's phone on the screen. Agatha asked him to show the calls she received on the day of her murder.

'There's a call there from her brother at four forty-five p.m.,' Simon said, pointing to the screen, 'and the only other call is also from him at five ten p.m.'

'Those are the two calls he and Miss Carstairs said they made,' Toni pointed out.

'Yes, I know,' Agatha said, thinking hard. 'Toni, can you check what time Anthony Feldrake and Mary Carstairs arrived at the Feathers and what time they left?' Toni made a note on her pad while Agatha continued. 'In the meantime, we need to look at Joan Feldrake's photo files, Simon.'

Pictures of birds and countryside appeared on the screen and Agatha asked Simon to scroll through them quickly until she spotted the ones she wanted. He clicked on the first of the batch and three naked people appeared on the screen.

'Blimey!' Patrick snorted, giving one of his rare laughs. 'I wasn't expecting that!'

Simon laughed, too, and on the far side of the room Mrs Freedman looked up from her paperwork, froze for a second and immediately looked back down again.

'Those look like blackmail photos to me,' John said.

'Shot from a distance without the subjects knowing,' Patrick said, nodding. 'I think you're right.'

'I agree,' Agatha said, 'but who was Joan Feldrake blackmailing? I've no idea who those people are.'

'I do,' Toni said, standing and stepping forward in what looked like an action replay of her Stevie Sexton moment. She pointed to the woman on the screen. 'They're Joan Feldrake's other neighbours. That's Mrs Bellingham. I don't know who the man on top of her is . . .'

'But she looks like she's enjoying herself,' Roy said, turning his head sideways for a better view.

'. . . and the man standing watching with a beer in his hand,' Toni went on, 'is Mr Bellingham.'

'I get it now,' Agatha said. 'I knew the place looked a bit familiar. The thing down the edge of the photo that looks like a tree is actually the camouflage at the side of Joan Feldrake's birdwatching hide. She used her hide to get photos of her neighbours!'

'That would explain why their complaints about the

182

hide were suddenly dropped,' Patrick said. 'She threatened to humiliate them with these photos unless they stopped.'

'They told me they were her best friends,' Toni said. 'They even claimed to have keys to her place so they could deal with any problems whenever she was away.'

'That's exactly what you would want your neighbours to do,' Agatha said, 'and with these photos in her possession, Joan Feldrake could make sure her neighbours did as she wanted. She was able to control them as she pleased. I'm guessing they used their keys to get in and search the house, doubtless looking for a device or photo card of some kind where she'd stored these pictures.'

'Would they really care enough to kill her, though?' asked Roy. 'I mean, if Mrs Bellingham enjoyed having sex with men who weren't her husband and he enjoyed watching, it's a bit weird but it's not illegal between consenting adults, is it?'

'Mrs Bellingham is a nurse,' Patrick said, consulting his notes, 'and Mr Bellingham is an operating theatre technician. They both work at Mircester General. If these photos were posted on the internet or emailed to anyone at the hospital, they would be ridiculed. It would make it very difficult for them to work normally with everyone talking about them and sniggering behind their backs. I'd say their livelihoods were at stake.'

'If they were threatened with losing their income and facing financial ruin,' John pointed out, 'that definitely gives them a motive for murder.'

'Maybe for the murder of Miss Feldrake,' Toni said,

'but what about Miss Smart? What links the Bellinghams to her?'

'On the day she died, Stella Smart told me Joan Feldrake's murder was "all about money and revenge" and that the murderers would be coming for her next,' Agatha said. 'If she was in on a blackmail scam that involved the Bellinghams handing over cash as well as doing as they were told, then that could explain a lot. Patrick, see what strings you can pull to find out about the Bellinghams' finances and if they were making regular payments to Feldrake or Smart.'

'"Money and revenge" are powerful motives, but they could also apply to the Boddingtons and Alan Trimble,' Roy pointed out.

'They could,' Agatha agreed, 'which makes it all the more important to check out their alibis.'

Agatha consulted her own notepad for a second before turning to Simon again.

'One last thing from the phones,' she said. 'Find a message between Joan Feldrake and Stella Smart about "the SS legacy", please, Simon.'

Simon quickly found the correct message and frowned at it when he read it on screen.

'"He's desecrating the SS legacy"?' he said, thoroughly confused. 'Have we got something about Nazis coming into the case now?'

'I thought that for a moment, too,' Agatha agreed, 'but that's just too bizarre . . .'

'It's nothing to do with Nazis,' Toni said. 'SS is Stevie Sexton. They were out to get rid of Eric Spalding!'

'Of course!' Agatha slapped her hand against her

184

thigh. 'They idolised Stevie Sexton when they were young. They would hate what Spalding was doing with his tribute act.'

'Joan Feldrake's complaints to the council didn't stop him,' Patrick said.

'And if they'd got wind of his drugs operation and were threatening to expose him,' John said, 'he'd have a perfect motive for murder.'

'You need to finish your report, Simon,' Agatha said, holding her head in her hands, 'but we're not submitting it yet or handing over Spalding to the police. He's just rocketed up our suspects list. So far, we haven't really eliminated anyone and the only suspect in this case we know for sure didn't do it is me!'

Agatha organised her team. Simon was finishing his report and checking Trimble's and the Boddingtons' alibis. Patrick started looking into the Bellinghams' finances. Toni was trying to establish precisely when Anthony Feldrake and Mary Carstairs left the Feathers. John tried talking to former police colleagues to find out who else was in the traffic jam caused by the fallen tree. Any of them might have seen something that could identify who killed Joan Feldrake. Agatha and Roy then worked with John to follow up on the traffic jam names.

By the end of the afternoon, very little progress had been made and Agatha left the office with John feeling tired and frustrated. She drove them home to Carsely, parked the car and they headed to the Red Lion, intent on relaxing with a drink and a bite to eat. As they were about to enter the pub, Agatha heard her name being called and turned, almost falling over a chalk board that had been set out on the pavement advertising for catering and bar staff.

'I'm sorry, Mrs Raisin, I didn't mean to startle you,' Gethin Fawkes said, walking towards them. 'I just wanted to make sure you were all right after that business yesterday.'

'I'm fine, thanks, Mr Fawkes,' Agatha replied.

'You can call me Gethin,' he said, smiling. 'Seems silly to be so formal when I've seen so much of you lately . . . Oh! I didn't mean . . .!' He waved a hand down his torso, a panicked look crossing his face.

'Don't worry, Gethin,' she said, laughing. 'I know what you meant.'

'Would you like to join us for a drink?' John asked, looking towards the pub door.

'No, I won't, but thanks, anyway,' he said, holding up an envelope. 'I bought a card at Harvey's and wrote a note to Mrs Bloxby to apologise for ruining the Ladies Society meeting last Friday. I just want to drop it off at the vicarage.'

'That's really sweet of you,' Agatha said, 'but I don't think you ruined the evening. You added a real touch of drama for everyone there.'

'It's not right, me acting like that,' he said, looking down at the pavement, ashamed. 'I spoke to my . . . Well, what I mean is, I need to pull myself together. Those two ladies being killed on my land . . . and then what happened to you . . . It's made me see that things need to change. *I* need to change – and it starts with this.' He held up the envelope, and looked from Agatha to John and back again.

'I'm sure Mrs Bloxby will be very pleased to see you, Gethin,' Agatha said, and Gethin Fawkes hurried off in the direction of St Jude's.

Agatha and John took a table by the window looking out over the street and John went to the bar, returning with two menus, a glass of red wine for Agatha and a tall glass of sparkling water for himself.

'You didn't fancy some wine?' she asked.

'I've been feeling a bit out of sorts,' he explained, placing his glass on the table. 'This will do me for now.'

It didn't take them long to browse the limited menu, John choosing shepherd's pie and Agatha opting for lasagne. She knew it would be pre-prepared, probably frozen and either reheated in a scorching oven or nuked in the microwave, but, given that her expectations were fairly low, she didn't expect to be disappointed. Secretly, she was looking forward to polishing it all off and then sampling the crispy bits stuck to the edge of the dish which she could chip off with a spoon, as she had done so many times before.

'Gethin Fawkes seemed nothing like the angry man you described from the church hall meeting,' John commented.

'He didn't, did he?' Agatha agreed. 'I'm inclined to think that threatening to "exterminate" the twitchers was just a moment of madness. The thing is, if Gethin – or him and an accomplice – murdered those two women, why would he place himself at the scene of Stella Smart's murder by pulling me out of the water? If he

187

was involved in the killings, he would just have walked away. Neither Roy nor I would have seen him. Instead, he saved my life.'

'I think Gethin Fawkes has just dropped to the bottom of the suspect list,' John said.

'I think so, too. Losing your temper doesn't make you a murderer. I've got a bit of a temper myself but . . .'

'You do?' John said, raising his eyebrows and smiling. 'Can't say I'd ever noticed.'

'Careful,' Agatha said, giving him a playful warning, 'you don't want to set me off. There's still that barn, though,' she went on. 'He's very secretive about that.'

'A bit like having a temper,' John said, 'having a secret doesn't make you a killer.'

'No, you're right,' Agatha said, having made up her mind. 'Gethin Fawkes may have been our prime suspect at one time, but not any more. I don't believe he's a murderer.'

Having finished their meal, they strolled along Carsely High Street towards Lilac Lane in the early-evening sunshine. Then John's phone rang. The call was brief and he looked concerned.

'That was Bill Wong,' he said. 'Wilkes has got wind of the incident at the church hall. He's set out to arrest Gethin Fawkes.'

'We have to warn him!' Agatha said, quickening her pace and reaching for her phone.

'You have his number?' John asked.

'No, but I know a man who does,' she replied, hitting

a speed dial button. 'Gustav? Don't mess me about. I need to talk to Charles.'

'Sir Charles is in the kitchen,' Gustav said, in an uncharacteristic, plaintive whine. 'He's helping that Roberts woman cook dinner! We have to do something, Mrs Raisin! This is all becoming totally outrageous!'

'I need a number for Gethin Fawkes, Gustav!' Agatha demanded. 'It's urgent!'

'I have it here,' he said, reciting the number from Charles's contact list. 'But you must promise me, you'll—'

Agatha rang off and called Gethin Fawkes.

'There's no answer,' she said. By now they had almost reached her car. 'The farm's not far. Let's go there now. I have to warn him about Wilkes. I owe him that much.'

'I'll drive,' John said, and Agatha passed him her car keys. 'You keep trying his phone.'

It took them just a few minutes to reach the road off which ran the track to Fawkes's farm. John pointed to two cars coming down the track.

'Those are Mircester CID cars,' he said. 'Looks like we're too late.'

'Slow down,' Agatha said, 'and drive past.'

As they got closer, they could see Wilkes sitting in the passenger seat of one of the cars, and Fawkes, flanked by two plain-clothes officers, sitting in the back of the other.

'We're too late,' John said.

'Keep going,' Agatha told him. 'They'll take the road back towards Carsely. We can turn just up ahead.'

John pulled off the road at the entrance to a field and turned the car around.

'Take the track up to Fawkes's farm,' Agatha said. 'This could be our chance to have a look around.'

'I thought he'd gone to the bottom of the suspect list,' John said.

'He has,' Agatha confirmed, 'and this is our chance to drop him off completely, whatever that fool Wilkes thinks.'

They pulled up outside the farmhouse and walked up to the door, Agatha rapping the brass knocker. The door creaked slightly open.

'Hello?' she called. 'Is anyone home?'

There was no reply. They pushed the door open and walked into an orderly kitchen that appeared to take up most of the ground floor. The flagstones underfoot were scrubbed and brushed clean, as was the wooden table in the middle of the room. Pots and pans hung in regimented rows above a tidy work surface beside an immaculately clean stove. Moving further into the kitchen, Agatha opened cupboard doors and drawers to find clean crockery and cutlery, all neatly stacked and arranged. A deep, white 'Belfast' sink sat below a window that looked out towards the small barn. To its right was a wooden door that Agatha assumed led to the rest of the house.

'He likes to keep everything shipshape,' John noted.

'He certainly does,' Agatha said, feeling slightly guilty that her kitchen could only ever come close to competing with this one immediately after one of Doris Simpson's Tuesday visits. 'Even James would be impressed, and everything in his place is always immaculate.'

She then felt, as much as heard, a low rumbling sound. Her hand touched her tummy, but she knew it couldn't be hunger grumbles. She'd had lasagne and garlic bread in the Red Lion. Then she heard the sound again and looked over towards the entrance where Molly, Fawkes's collie, was crouched in the doorway, softly growling.

'I should have expected Molly would be here,' Agatha said quietly, standing shoulder-to-shoulder with John. Molly's brown eyes were fixed on them, unblinking.

'It's like she's trying to hypnotise us,' John said and they shuffled sideways together, putting the table between Molly and themselves. Molly advanced into the room, hugging the floor in a commando crawl, ready to dart left or right should Agatha or John move. She then froze, poised for action.

'She doesn't look too dangerous, really,' John reasoned.

'There are lots of nasty sharp teeth in that cute little face,' Agatha warned him. 'We'll never make it past her to that door. She's faster than us.'

'I think she's smarter than us as well,' John decided.

'We can make it to the other door if we're quick,' Agatha said, her eyes flitting to the door near the sink.

'Okay, let's go on the count of three,' John said, reaching out slowly to grasp a copper kettle from an ornate Welsh dresser. 'Maybe I can distract her with this. One . . . two . . . three!'

John flung the copper pot in Molly's direction, knowing he had no chance of ever hitting her, but it made her take her eyes off them while she dodged it and they bounded three paces to the door. It opened onto a cosy living room, with a staircase to the upper floor on their right. John slammed the door behind them and they heard Molly's claws scrabbling on the other side.

'We can get back to the car that way,' Agatha said, indicating a door to their left.

They sprinted outside, only to see Molly shoot out from the corner of the house and crouch low on a patch of grass, having run round to intercept them.

'Snakes and bastards!' Agatha hissed. 'She's cut us off! Quick, this way – into the barn!'

They ran full tilt to the small barn, heaved open the door and slammed it shut just in time to hear Molly arrive and let out a bark of frustration. The barn was in darkness, with just a small gap at the foot of the door allowing a ground-level slither of daylight to slip through. On the other side of the gap, they could see Molly's paws pacing to and fro. Then they heard her snuffling, her nose crammed into the gap. She let out another rumbling growl.

'What the hell are we going to do now?' Agatha groaned. 'She's got us trapped!'

Chapter Nine

Agatha backed away from the barn door, her eyes growing accustomed to the gloom, although only enough to make out vague shapes in the darkness. John took out his phone and switched on its flashlight.

'There must be a proper light in here somewhere,' he said, scanning the walls for a switch. Eventually he found it, high on the right side of the door. He clicked it on.

There was a pinging sound and flickers of light as a series of four large fluorescent lights suspended from the high ceiling stuttered into life. A moment later, the barn was as bright as the day outside.

'There must be another way out,' Agatha said, scanning the barn. Various items of farm machinery were stored systematically around the walls, each evidently in its own allocated space, some covered with tarpaulins. Between them, filling spaces on the walls, were racks of tools, as many as Agatha had ever seen in any garage workshop, all stored methodically by type and size.

'Tidiest barn I've ever been in,' John said. 'Most farms are like organised chaos, but this place is almost obsessively neat.'

'There's another door over there!' Agatha cried, rushing over to try the latch. It was locked tight.

'Padlocked from the outside, I'd say,' John observed.

'And even if it wasn't,' Agatha said, pointing to the tip of a paw that had appeared under the door, 'Molly's tracked us to this side of the barn without even being able to see us.'

'Dogs can scent and hear better than they can see,' John said. 'I think Molly will know precisely where we are while we're in here.'

Agatha looked at her phone.

'I've got no signal,' she said. 'How about you?'

'Not a squeak,' he replied. 'That probably explains why Gethin didn't answer his phone. This area has really patchy reception.'

'Maybe if we could get up a bit higher, we could call for help,' Agatha suggested. 'That worked for me the time I was trapped in the ice-cream company freezer room, remember?'

They used a ladder they found to try as many different high points in the barn as they could, but to no avail. An hour later, they sat down on a hay bale together to figure out another plan.

'Even if we'd got a phone signal,' John said, 'who would we have called?'

'Any of my team would come straight to the rescue,' Agatha said. 'All they'd have to do is distract Molly with a sausage or throw a net over her or something.'

'If we want to make a break for it,' John suggested, 'there are plenty of things in here we could use to fight her off.'

194

'We can't harm Molly,' Agatha insisted. 'Gethin might be trying to turn over a new leaf, but he'll flip it right back again if we injure his dog.'

'We don't have to hurt her,' John said. 'We only need to find a way to keep her at bay until we can get to the car.'

'It can't hurt to try,' Agatha said, getting to her feet and grabbing a dust sheet covering something large and bulky in the middle of the floor. 'Let's see what's under here.'

'Leave that alone!' Gethin Fawkes suddenly roared from the barn door. 'What the blazes are you doing in here?'

'We came to warn you that Wilkes was coming for you,' Agatha said.

'But we were too late,' John explained, 'and Molly chased us in here. We've been trying to figure out a way to get past her ever since.'

Fawkes stared at Agatha, then at John, then his shoulders seemed to relax. Molly, on the other hand, had flattened herself against the floor of the barn, growling at them both.

'I suppose you meant well,' Fawkes grunted. 'Outside, Molly!'

The dog turned and shot out of the barn, taking up a new guard post in the evening sunshine, looking in through the door to keep her eyes pinned on Agatha and John at all times.

'Wilkes didn't hold you in custody for very long,' Agatha said. 'You got off far lighter than us.'

'He'd no right to take me in at all,' Fawkes grumbled.

'Complete waste of time. I was at a farm on the other side of Evesham the day Miss Feldrake died. There were at least twenty people there bidding for machinery that was being sold off. Any one of them could vouch for me, and as soon as that Sergeant Wong could get hold of them on the phone, three of them did. I wasn't in the police station more than half an hour.'

'This is the cleanest, tidiest barn we've ever seen,' Agatha said, looking round the space. 'I know it's a private place for you, but I don't understand why.'

Fawkes stared at the ground, just as he had done outside the Red Lion, but this time he didn't seem embarrassed or ashamed; he was obviously thinking, considering his options.

'Sit down,' he said to them, pointing to the hay bale, having made up his mind. 'I keep this place private because it's special to me, but if I'm going to make changes, then maybe this is one of them.'

He took hold of the dust sheet Agatha had been about to lift, and dragged it gently to one side, revealing a gleaming, red, vintage tractor.

'This is a nineteen fifty-one David Brown Cropmaster,' Fawkes explained. 'It was my father's machine but when Rhiannon and I . . . Rhiannon was my wife. She died . . .' Fawkes paused for a moment, taking a deep breath.

'Gethin, you don't have to—' Agatha began, but he held up a hand to stop her.

'No, it's time I . . . time I sorted myself out,' he said, 'and this is part of it. Come and take a look.'

Never having taken any interest in tractors or any other kind of agricultural machinery, Agatha surprised

196

herself by seeing the old Cropmaster almost like a living thing. It had curves and graceful lines that she found quite delightful. It still had big wheels with huge tyres, but it was far smaller than modern tractors and looked far more elegant. It helped that it wasn't covered in the kind of mud – and worse – that was splattered over the enormous tractors she got stuck behind when driving on the roads around Carsely. There was scarcely even a speck of dust on the red Cropmaster.

'It's absolutely gorgeous, Gethin,' she said, standing on tiptoe to look at the open driving position, 'and it has two seats, side-by-side.'

'Rhiannon and I used to sit there together,' he said, 'when we were newly married and came here to live with my old dad. She loved riding on the tractor. We'd drive it up the hill to where we had a picnic spot. You can see six counties from up there. We were never happier. Shortly after my dad died, the Cropmaster conked out. It wasn't up to the job any more anyway, so we parked it in here and over the years it gathered rust and dust.

'I always told Rhiannon I'd rebuild it one day and we'd ride it up the hill again, but we never got the chance. Always too busy with one thing and another. Then, when Rhiannon passed, I swore I'd restore the Cropmaster and I've been working on it ever since.'

John walked round the tractor, admiring the job Fawkes had done and complimenting him on his fine work. Agatha looked down beside the engine, where there was a shelf on which sat the tractor's battery. Standing on the battery was a picture frame containing a photograph of a younger, happier Fawkes posing with a young woman.

'Is that Rhiannon?' she asked, and he nodded. 'She's beautiful, Gethin.'

He sat down on the hay bale, bowed his head and trawled his hands through his hair.

'I come in here to talk to her,' he said, looking up at Agatha and John standing by the tractor. 'You probably think I'm mad, but I come in here to talk to Rhiannon. I try to keep everything on the farm the way she'd like it – the way we liked it – and talking to her helps to get me through the day. Crazy, eh?'

'No, mate,' John said. 'Not crazy at all.'

'Not in the slightest,' Agatha agreed. 'She'd be proud of the way you've kept the farm going – and over the moon about your father's old tractor.'

'But sometimes I get so angry,' he said, wringing his hands, 'and she'd be ashamed of me.'

'Nobody's perfect, Gethin,' Agatha said. 'She wouldn't be ashamed of you. She'd be proud. She'd certainly be very proud of you for saving me from drowning in that river.'

'Don't be so hard on yourself,' John said. 'I'm sure Rhiannon wouldn't want that. She'd want you to be happy.'

'I reckon you're right,' Fawkes said, standing up, holding his head high. 'I figured that out for myself. Hearing you say it makes it doubly true. That's why things will be different. That's what she would want and that's what I aim to do.'

They left the barn together, Molly trotting meekly at Fawkes's heel.

Agatha woke that night alone. That wasn't usually such a strange thing, but John had stayed over and he wasn't lying there beside her. The empty space in the bed was what had woken her. James used to do that when we were married, she thought to herself – wake in the night and go next door to his own bed in his own house. John, however, was nothing like James. Something was wrong. She slipped on a robe and went downstairs.

She found John sitting at the kitchen table with a cup of tea in front of him.

'Sorry,' he said, smiling. 'Didn't mean to disturb you. I couldn't sleep.'

'But you were so tired,' Agatha said, sitting beside him. 'You were looking forward to a good night's sleep.'

'I know, but there's so much buzzing round in my head,' he said. 'Somebody tried to kill you and whoever it was is still out there. You were arrested and so was I. I know that's Wilkes's nonsense, but I had an exemplary record as a police officer and it still rankles . . . I still feel the disgrace. Then there's the whole cruise line thing and, of course, there's a double murderer still on the loose, and—'

'Well, at least we've reduced the suspects list on that by one – Gethin didn't do it.'

'I know, and I've been thinking about Gethin, too,' John said. 'He's been so unhappy for so long. If anything should happen to one of us, we won't be like that, will we? The other one will carry on, right? The other one will be happy – no wasted years. Promise?'

'Of course I promise,' she said, reaching out to hold his hand, 'but nothing's going to happen to us. Come on – come back to bed. Try to get some sleep.'

She kissed him on the forehead, put her arm around him and they went back upstairs together.

The following morning, Agatha and John arrived at Raisin Investigations to find that the previous afternoon's frustrating and apparently fruitless inquiries were actually starting to show results. Roy was sitting at the spare desk in the outer office with a notepad, having established himself as a temporary member of the team.

'I finally got hold of most of the people in the other cars at the scene of the Feldrake murder,' he reported. 'They were all terribly nice but, basically, none of them saw anything that you didn't see. The only ones I haven't spoken to were in Bill Wong's report and they didn't see anything either.'

'The other cars . . .' Agatha said, picturing the scene in her head, then dismissing it again. 'Well, I suppose we didn't really expect much from them.'

'I spoke to a contact at Mircester General,' Patrick said. 'He couldn't tell me exactly how much the Bellinghams are paid, but he did say it was common knowledge that they take on as much overtime as they can get to boost their earnings.'

'That would make sense if Feldrake and Smart had been blackmailing them,' John said. 'They'd need as much money as they could get their hands on.'

'That's true,' Patrick agreed, 'but I also found posts

from Mrs Bellingham on social media.' He turned his computer screen to the room to show photographs of the Bellinghams on exotic holidays. 'They've had recent holidays in Jamaica and Cancun in Mexico. It seems they like to visit hotels and beach clubs where the guests are quite . . . liberal-minded.'

'Swingers' clubs!' Simon whooped. 'Cool!'

'That's their choice, of course,' Agatha said, frowning at Simon, 'but people who have blackmailers trying to screw every penny out of them don't tend to splash out on expensive, long-haul holidays.'

'And apparently they're at home today,' Patrick said, 'packing for a flight to Thailand tomorrow. Mrs Bellingham's been talking about practically nothing else at work for the past couple of weeks.'

'They could be fleeing the country,' Toni suggested.

'Possible, but unlikely,' Agatha said. 'I think the Bellinghams have dropped way down the suspects list. They may have peculiar habits, but I doubt murder's one of them. Anyone else?'

'I played football last night with some mates,' Simon said. 'One of them is dating a girl who works at Boddington's. We met her in the pub afterwards and she told me that the Boddingtons and Trimble have been in the office twenty-four/seven. The security cameras in the building would confirm that.'

'There are always ways to avoid cameras,' Agatha pointed out.

'Sure,' Simon said, nodding, 'but some of the staff have been in the office working long hours, too. They were promised extra time off rather than overtime pay. She was one of them and she says Mr and Mrs Boddington as well as Alan Trimble were at their desks when both Joan Feldrake and Stella Smart were killed.'

'That rules out the Boddington connection,' John said.

'Which leaves us with Anthony Feldrake and Mary Carstairs, or our drugs dealer, Eric Spalding,' Agatha said, imagining the houses in Tweeting Bottom.

'I went to the Feathers last night and talked to a waitress who was working last Saturday,' Toni said. 'She said she thinks Mary Carstairs and Anthony Feldrake arrived about four thirty. She knows they left only half an hour later at five p.m. because that's when she came off shift and saw them driving out of the car park down towards Ancombe Vale.'

'Is that so?' Agatha mused. 'I need to have a think about their movements on the day. You know, I think we're actually making progress. I get the feeling we're closing in. Anything more on Spalding?'

'He has a van and a motorbike registered to him,' Patrick said with a shrug. 'That's about all I've got.'

'He definitely has a motorbike,' Toni confirmed. 'I saw his crash helmet in his hall.'

'I also heard back from my old mate in Scotland about Anthony Feldrake,' Patrick said. 'The rumour is that he was sacked for skiving. Oil rigs are big, complex structures with lots of little nooks and crannies that are hidden, well out of sight. Seems Feldrake had stowed blankets in a couple of places so that he could sneak off, curl up and have a nap or read the paper, leaving everyone else to get on with the work. Nobody ever knew where he was. Eventually, he was found out and sacked.'

'For a lazybones, he's been pretty active sorting out his sister's affairs,' Simon commented.

'His wife's divorcing him,' Roy said, 'he's got no job, no income and no money. He's desperate, and desperate people do desperate things – including murder!'

'Well, that's possible,' Agatha said. 'Right now, I want eyes on our remaining suspects. Simon, Toni, get out to Tweeting Bottom. Don't go into the development – you'll be spotted straight away. Set yourself up in the field on the other side of the main road. Find a vantage point where you can see the Feldrake house and Spalding's place. You should be able to do that with field glasses or that monocular thingy. We need to know if they're at home.'

Simon and Toni left the office, Patrick went back to his regular work and Roy, with nothing much else to do, went shopping. John checked a message on his phone.

'I need to go home and do some paperwork for the cruise line,' he said. 'They can delay me joining the ship until the next trip.'

'That's good news,' Agatha said, beaming an enthusiastic smile. 'I'll let you know if anything happens here.'

Mrs Freedman then handed Agatha a copy of that morning's *Mircester Telegraph*, which led with the headline: 'Private Eye Arrested on Suspicion of Murder'.

'Well, she had to do it before the nationals got hold of it,' Agatha said, looking at Charlotte Clark's byline. 'At least this way I'll get to have my own say in the press eventually. If we get calls from any other reporters, Helen, tell them I'm not available for comment. In any case, any comments they got from me would be unprintable . . .'

Agatha settled herself in her office, writing notes on a pad and trying to think her way through the events leading up to Joan Feldrake's death. She was confident that, if she could piece all of it together logically, she'd see what she was sure she was missing. She was still puzzling over it all when she saw the first of the morning's unexpected visitors arrive. DCI Wilkes appeared in the outer office and Mrs Freedman stood in front of him, barring the way to Agatha's room. Agatha called her off, inviting Wilkes in to avoid Patrick getting involved. Patrick squaring up to Wilkes would mean tempers getting frayed and Wilkes having an excuse to cause more trouble.

'You probably know I had Gethin Fawkes in custody yesterday,' Wilkes said, standing in the doorway to Agatha's office, having been invited in but not to sit down.

'Why would I know that?' Agatha asked, as innocently as she could manage, perching casually on the corner of her desk.

'Because you tried to call him several times, Mrs Raisin,' Wilkes sneered. 'I have his phone records. Why were you calling him?'

'I wanted to thank him properly for saving my life,' Agatha said. It wasn't entirely a lie. Had she got through to Gethin, she undoubtedly would have done so.

'Rubbish!' Wilkes said, with a slimy smile. 'You phoned because you are in league with him! You were there when he issued threats against Joan Feldrake and

Stella Smart at the church hall. You were there when Feldrake was killed and you were there when Smart was killed.'

'I'm glad to see you've finally got round to linking their murders,' Agatha said, folding her arms. 'You're catching up slowly, but you're headed in the wrong direction. I had nothing to do with either of the killings.'

'Yes, you did,' Wilkes said, shaking his head. 'All I need is the one piece of the jigsaw that makes it all fit together, then I've got you! I reckon I'm this close to finding it!' He held out his right hand, showing the tips of his thumb and forefinger with a tiny space between them.

'What's that?' Agatha asked. 'The size of the pea brain that rattles around inside your head? Find evidence on me? Fat chance! You couldn't find your arse with both hands, Wilkes – now bugger off out of my office before I call a real policeman!'

Wilkes made to say something, failed to find the words, snorted, turned on his heel and left. No sooner had Agatha sat back down at her desk to work in peace and quiet, however, than her phone rang. It was Gustav.

'Mrs Raisin,' he said, 'please have the courtesy not to cut me off again. I need your help. I am sorely worried about Sir Charles and this woman. We need to do something. His behaviour is becoming quite ridiculous!'

'What's he done now?' Agatha asked.

'He's following her around the house like a loyal little puppy!' Gustav sounded truly appalled. 'He's even said he'll take her shopping later this morning! He never goes shopping! I have always done all the shopping!'

'Shopping?' Agatha was intrigued. 'Where are they going shopping?'

'Carsely!' Gustav whined. 'Who on earth goes shopping in Carsely? There are hardly any shops. Why would he take her there?'

'Why indeed?' Agatha replied, pondering this latest, unlikely development. 'All right, Gustav. Calm down and leave this with me.'

Agatha sat for a few minutes gathering her thoughts, then she plucked her handbag out of its drawer and headed out.

'Helen, if anyone wants me, they can get me on my mobile,' she said, crossing the outer office and skipping downstairs to the street.

Agatha headed home, but took a detour to the Feathers, pulling into the car park, where there were only three other cars, and taking in her surroundings. Ancombe was one of those Cotswold villages that seemed almost too perfect to be real. It was the sort of place that, should someone be making a Hollywood movie set in a Cotswold village, the producers would insist on rebuilding, stone for stone, in California. It had a three-hundred-year-old well in the shape of a skull built on an ancient spring, a village shop, a church, the prettiest collection of thatched cottages imaginable and the pub, the Feathers. Ancombe attracted tourists in the way that Carsely did not, and Agatha was glad about that. Carsely might not win a village beauty contest, but neither was it plagued with busloads of day trippers.

She drove out of the car park and down the gentle hill to the bridge that had been the site of her dramatic rescue, then over the bridge to park once again in the lay-by immediately beyond where the tree had fallen. She sat in her car, pushing the button that lowered the driver's window. It had taken her less than four minutes to drive from the Feathers. With no one else in sight and no passing traffic, she breathed in the sweet, damp smell of the woodland. There was something here she couldn't see, niggling her like an itch she couldn't scratch, but she drove off after a couple of minutes, inspiration having eluded her.

At home in Lilac Lane, she had barely had enough time to make herself a cup of coffee before her doorbell rang. She opened the door to find Sir Charles Fraith standing there.

'Charles, what a surprise,' she said, not sounding in the least surprised. 'Come in. Let's have a coffee and a seat in the garden.'

'I was just passing, really,' Charles said, following her up the hall. 'I brought Mrs Roberts into the village for a spot of shopping. Stocking up on essentials, that sort of thing.'

'Really?' Agatha said, pouring him a cup of coffee from the pot. 'I wouldn't have thought shopping for essentials was your sort of thing.'

'Well, I feel I have to give poor Shona – that's Mrs Roberts – a hand now and then,' he explained.

'You don't need to give her a hand, Charles,' Agatha

said as they sat in the sunshine. 'What you do need to do is to give me credit for a little intelligence.'

'I . . . I . . . don't know what you mean,' he stammered.

'Yes you do,' Agatha insisted. 'You know exactly what I mean. I don't like being played, Charles. You're not the first person recently I've had to warn about that. Your little game with Mrs Roberts is really quite pathetic. You knew that if you started acting out of character and fawning all over someone who is supposed to be one of your staff, Gustav would be horrified. It would be totally unacceptable for him to let you make a fool of yourself with a domestic, even if that's probably what your ancestors have been getting up to for centuries.'

'What's Gustav got to do with this?' Charles asked.

'Everything!' Agatha snapped. 'Whenever Gustav has a problem with you that he can't handle on his own, who does he turn to? Me, that's who! You knew he'd call me sooner or later, and that's absolutely what you wanted. You wanted me to think that you had fallen for Mrs Roberts. I'm not sure whether you expected that I would be consumed with jealousy or simply see it as an irresistible challenge to fight off the other woman and get you back in my life, but whichever one it was, you were wrong on both counts!'

At that moment, the doorbell rang and Agatha walked through the house to answer it. Mrs Roberts stood on the doorstep.

'I'm sorry to bother you, Mrs Raisin,' she said and, for the first time, Agatha noticed a lilting Scottish accent. Then she realised that she'd never heard the woman speak more than about three words before.

'Sir Charles told me he would be here and I should call round when I'd got all these things.' She held up two carrier bags.

'He is here, Mrs Roberts,' Agatha said and watched a frown etch itself on the younger woman's face.

'I hate that name,' she said. 'It's not my name any more. I'm Shona MacNeil. They're forever calling me Roberts up at the big house.'

'They're a bit stuck in their ways at Barfield,' Agatha agreed.

'Well, they can get stuck in their ways without me . . .' she said, just as Charles appeared in the hall.

'Shona,' he said, 'you sound upset . . .'

'Not me,' she said. 'I'm not upset. I feel fine. Here are your groceries.' She put the bags down in the hall. 'I must go now. I won't be coming back to the big house with you. I've been offered a job in the Red Lion cooking and tending the bar. There's a flat above the pub and they need someone straight away. I'll call round to collect my things later. Goodbye, Sir Charles. Goodbye, Mrs Raisin. Sorry to have taken up your time.'

'No need for apologies, Miss MacNeil,' Agatha said. 'I'll see you next time I pop into the pub!'

Shona MacNeil left for the Red Lion and Agatha sat down on her staircase. She looked up at Charles and burst out laughing.

'I'm sorry, Charles,' she said, calming herself. 'I'm not really laughing at you. Well, I suppose I am a bit! It's only that I've never seen any scheme fall so completely apart in one fell swoop!'

'It's me who should apologise,' he said with a heavy

sigh. 'I should have known better. I should treat you with far more respect.'

'Yes, you should!' Agatha couldn't stop herself laughing again. 'I should be furious, but it's just so funny the way your little plot has totally backfired.'

'You can't blame me for trying,' he said, shrugging and picking up his bags of shopping, managing a smile and a bit of a laugh as he did so.

'Stop trying, Charles,' she told him. 'We need each other as friends. That's the way it should be.'

'Maybe it should,' he agreed, 'but I can't promise I'll ever stop trying.'

Toni was standing behind a tree in the field opposite Tweeting Bottom, with Simon concealed in some bushes off to her left, when she put in a call to Agatha.

'We're in position,' Toni said. 'We've watched the Bellinghams loading one suitcase into their car. From what we can see through their windows, they're packing another.'

'What about Feldrake and Carstairs?' Agatha asked.

'Anthony Feldrake's car and his sister's car are both in the driveway,' Toni reported. 'I think I spotted Carstairs in the garden earlier and I think I saw Feldrake going into the house when he drove up earlier.'

'You think?' Agatha wasn't impressed with the uncertainty.

'Well, I've never met them,' Toni pointed out. 'You've always dealt with Carstairs, and Feldrake wasn't home when I went door-to-door here.'

'He wasn't . . .' Agatha started to hear alarm bells ringing.

'Eric Spalding is definitely there,' Toni went on. 'He seems to have taken a break right now but we've seen him loading stuff out of his garage into his van.'

'What sort of stuff?' asked Agatha.

'We can't really tell,' Toni said. 'The back doors are wide open but we can't see the rear of it because it's parked facing this way.'

There was a long pause. For a moment Toni thought she'd lost the connection.

'Agatha, are you still there?' Toni asked.

'Yes, yes, of course,' Agatha replied, 'why wouldn't I be? Toni, keep watch on the lot of them. Let me know immediately if any of them leaves Tweeting Bottom. I can't stress how important this is.'

'I'll let you know,' Toni assured her, 'but why is it so important?'

'Because I think you just cracked the case!' Agatha announced. 'Now I need to go. I have to get John and Bill Wong and . . .'

Agatha's voice trailed away as if she had rung off while hurrying out of her house, which is precisely what she had done. She called Bill Wong as soon as she got to her car, using the car's hands-free gadgetry.

'Bill, how many officers can you get together for a raid this afternoon?' she asked.

'I'm not sure, Agatha,' he said. 'We've got people spread out all over the county. There's a lot going on today. What's this all about?'

'What would you say if I told you we could help you

nail a drugs dealer and the ringleader of the shoplifting gang that's been plaguing Mircester,' she said, 'and solve the murders of Joan Feldrake and Stella Smart into the bargain.'

'I'd say you'd gone potty,' Bill said with a short laugh, 'but because I'm talking to Agatha Raisin, I know I'd best take this seriously. I can pull a few off other jobs,' Bill said. 'If you say we can get a result here, I trust you. How about me and four uniforms?'

'That will have to do. Can you meet me in my office in ten minutes?'

'I'll be there, Agatha.'

She then called together her team and by the time she screeched to a halt, leaving her car parked half on the pavement outside Mr Tinkler's antiques shop in the lane below her office, they were all waiting for her. When she burst into the office, Mrs Freedman was wheeling a white board into the centre of the room, handing Agatha a marker pen instead of the customary coffee.

'Pay attention, everyone,' Agatha said, slinging her handbag on the back of Toni's chair. She sketched a plan of Tweeting Bottom on the board, matching names to the places as she went. 'This is Tweeting Bottom and this is the entrance. There's only one road in and it loops around a central green. Eric Spalding's house is here, next door to what was Joan Feldrake's house.

'If you go steaming in with your officers, Bill, Spalding will see you coming and he'll make a break for it. We know he has a motorbike, and if he gets out into the fields behind his house, we'll never catch him.

'I have Toni and Simon stationed here and here,' she

marked two crosses opposite the entrance to the development. Simon will stay in position. Everyone else will stay out of sight here, out on the main road. Toni and I will go in posing as researchers, which she has done before. We'll go to the Feldrake house first. They know I'm not a researcher, but we need their help. We'll warn them to expect visitors as we're mounting an operation against Spalding. We'll then visit Spalding. Simon will let you know when we go into his house.

'John, Roy and Patrick will then go to the Feldrake house to cover any back garden escape route. You and your officers can then come to Spalding's front door, Bill. You'll need to guard his van to stop him using that. When you ring the doorbell, we'll make our excuses to leave and you can rush in and slap the cuffs on him. What do you think?'

'As a plan,' said John, 'it's got more holes in it than my bath sponge, and it puts you and Toni in far too much danger, Agatha.'

'Well, we've been there before,' Agatha said, 'and we can handle it, especially with you lot backing us up.'

'Wilkes isn't going to like this,' Patrick said, looking to Bill.

'He'll go absolutely apeshit crazy,' Bill agreed. 'I can't wait to see it.'

Chapter Ten

Agatha and Toni walked up the front path to Joan Feldrake's house, Toni wearing the 'university' ID lanyard she used when she went door-to-door and Agatha also sporting one, hers identifying her as Angela Potts. When they rang the doorbell, it was answered by Mary Carstairs.

'Mrs Raisin!' Mary Carstairs looked shocked. 'I . . . I thought you were in jail!'

'Jail? Me?' Agatha looked mystified, then waved a hand as though recalling something trivial that had simply slipped her mind. 'Ah, you mean the arrest thing. That was all a bit of a mix-up by the police. In fact, we're now working with the police on another matter. This is my colleague, Toni Gilmour. May we come in for a second?'

Carstairs stepped aside, inviting them into the hall, whereupon Anthony Feldrake came bustling through from the kitchen.

'Who is it, Mary?' he asked, then spotted Agatha. 'Oh . . . it's you.'

'It certainly is, Mr Feldrake,' Agatha said, smiling. 'I was just about to explain to Miss Carstairs. We're working with Mircester Police. You see, we discovered that the man next door, Eric Spalding, has been receiving stolen goods and dealing in drugs. We need a little help from you to—'

'What are you talking about?' said Feldrake. 'How do we know any of that's true?'

'Sergeant Wong is running the operation,' Agatha said. 'I think you know him.'

'I've got him on the line for a video call,' Toni said, holding up her phone to show Bill on-screen. He assured Anthony Feldrake that what Agatha was telling him was true.

'It's all a bit of a last-minute thing,' Agatha explained. 'This could be our only chance to nail Spalding. All we need you to do is to let three of our people in when they come to your door shortly. They'll go through to your garden to cover the back of the houses in case Spalding makes a break for it that way.'

'Well, I . . . I suppose that's okay,' Feldrake said.

'Thank you so much, Mr Feldrake,' Agatha said. 'I know you must be so preoccupied with the funeral on Monday, but I can assure you this will all be over before you know it.'

'We have to go next door now,' Toni said, 'to distract Spalding while our people come in from the main road.'

With that, they left the Feldrake house and walked calmly up Spalding's garden path. He answered the doorbell after two rings.

'Sorry, I was in my soundproof— Oh, it's you again,' he said, smiling when he saw Toni.

'Yes, I hope you don't mind, Mr Spalding, but this

is my boss, Angela, and I desperately wanted to introduce her to you,' Toni said. 'You see, she's a huge Stevie Sexton fan and she simply wouldn't believe me when I told her you performed as Stevie!'

'You do look very like him,' Agatha said, eyeing Spalding left and right. 'A little more distinguished, perhaps – a little more handsome! Do you wear the sequined jumpsuits and the spangly platform shoes?' She clasped her hands together and flexed her knees as if this was the most exciting moment of her entire life.

'Well, yes, that's all part of the act . . .' Spalding said. 'I've actually got one of his original stage suits.'

'You do? Would you show us it?' Agatha begged. 'Oh, please do. It would mean the world to me!'

'I don't really have time at the moment,' Spalding said, then saw the look of adoration on Agatha's face, 'but I guess I can spare a few minutes.'

'They're in,' Simon said into his phone, and the figures waiting behind the hedgerow on the main road made their move. John, Patrick and Roy headed for the Feldrake house while Bill Wong and his officers made a beeline for Spalding's place. They were all on foot to avoid the sound of a car engine alerting Spalding.

Inside his house, Spalding led Agatha and Toni to the back room where a selection of gaudy, sparkling outfits in blue and red hung on a clothes rail.

'These are copies,' Spalding said, holding one of the suits against himself. 'The one in the suit hanger bag is an original.'

'They're amazing,' Agatha cooed, reaching out to touch the transparent hanger bag.

216

'What's your favourite Stevie song, then?' Spalding asked.

'Oh, it's . . . um . . .' Agatha hesitated, racking her brains for a song title.

'"Wake Me When It's Over"!' Toni said, with a forced laugh. 'She's just embarrassed because she's forever belting it out round the office.'

'That's a classic,' Spalding said, picking up a guitar. 'Come on, let's give it a go now. I'll start it off and you join in!'

'Oh, I really don't . . .' Agatha was starting to worry – she didn't have a clue how the song went – then the doorbell rang.

Spalding made his way to the front door but had barely opened it a crack when it burst in, sending him reeling backwards. He turned to run only to find Agatha standing in the narrow hallway, wielding his guitar like a club. An instant later, two burly officers had flattened him and expertly snapped handcuffs onto his wrists.

'You're not old enough,' Spalding grunted, looking at Agatha. 'I should have known . . .'

'I'll take that as some sort of compliment,' Agatha said. 'You, on the other hand, will be a lot older before you get to wear a sequinned jumpsuit again.'

The police radios crackled and through the open front door they watched a police car roll sedately into Tweeting Bottom. There was no siren, but its blue lights were flashing.

'That should set the curtains twitching!' Agatha smiled and walked round to the Feldrake house with Toni and Bill. Roy opened the door and they went into the front room, where Anthony Feldrake stood at the net curtains, transfixed by the blue lights.

'You got him, then?' Feldrake said.

'We did,' Bill said, nodding a greeting to John as he walked into the room. 'Looks to me like he has a garage full of stolen goods. My officers will go through the whole lot. I'm pretty sure we'll find a stash of drugs of some kind, too. Spalding will go down for handling stolen property and dealing drugs. Hopefully we'll find something that will lead us to his suppliers. Thank you for your help, Mr Feldrake, and you, Miss Carstairs.'

'We didn't really do anything,' said Carstairs.

'Oh, but you did, Mary,' Agatha said. 'You and Anthony did so much. You murdered Joan Feldrake, you murdered Stella Smart, and you tried to murder me!'

'What? You must be mad!' Feldrake objected. 'I didn't kill my own sister!'

'Maybe not you,' Agatha said, turning to Carstairs. 'You killed Joan, didn't you, Mary?'

Carstairs stared up at her from the sofa, where she was sitting, tense and anxious, at the very edge of the seat cushion. When Agatha looked her in the eye, she immediately gazed down at the carpet.

'Yes, I thought so,' Agatha said. 'You bludgeoned Joan with a tree branch, didn't you? And you,' she turned back to Feldrake, 'have a bit more bulk, so you shoved Stella into the river and held her under till she drowned. You'd have done the same to me, wouldn't you?'

'This is nonsense!' Feldrake raged. 'You can't prove a word of it!'

'Oh, I think we can, Anthony,' Agatha said. 'I think

218

I've got your whole plan figured out. I think that when everything went wrong for you up north – losing your job, your wife divorcing you and taking you for every penny you had, losing your home – you came back here with your tail between your legs. I doubt Joan would have had much sympathy for you but when you saw that the three old friends were still together, now three old spinsters, you thought you'd pick on the weakest link – Mary. But your old sweetheart turned out to be made of sterner stuff than you imagined, didn't she? Was it her who decided to make you seem more respectable – widowed and retired, rather than divorced and sacked? I think it probably was. She'd know that would sit better with people round here.

'You fired each other up with the injustice and the spite that had led to Stella and Joan breaking up your relationship all those years ago, and when Mary told you about Stella lording it over her by threatening to drop her from the will, the two of you hatched a nasty little plan together. Your aim was to have it all. Apart from the shares in Boddington's, everything that Stella and Joan had would come to you. All you had to do was to get rid of them.'

'Utter crap!' Feldrake spat.

'No it's not, Anthony,' Agatha replied calmly. 'Here's how it all went down. You sent a message to Joan about the magnolia warbler, knowing that she wouldn't be able to resist rushing down to the woods in Ancombe Vale. You couldn't use your own phone for that: Joan would recognise your number. I'm assuming you used a cheap, disposable phone. It's probably at the bottom of the river now.

'You had booked a table at the Feathers and arrived at four thirty. You then called Joan at four forty-five p.m. You told me it was to get her to join you at the Feathers, Mary, but really it was to make sure she was down in the woods. You said you called her again from the Feathers but we know you left there at five p.m. and the second call wasn't made until five ten p.m. It only takes four minutes to drive from the Feathers to Ancombe Vale, so you were already there when you phoned her for the second time.

'It must have been quite nerve-racking for you at the Feathers and on that short drive. You had to time things just right. You had to make sure Joan was in the woods looking for the warbler, but you also had to make a show of waiting for her at the restaurant. You knew she'd spend ages looking for the bird but there was always a chance that she might give up, maybe take the warbler message as some kind of prank. You needed her there so you could deal with her before Stella arrived, also looking for the warbler.

'I think the plan was then to kill Stella as well and dump both of their bodies in the river. That way it would look like they'd had an argument – they were famous for that, after all – got into a fight and fell into the river.

'That second phone call to Joan was to distract her, wasn't it? That way you could sneak up on her and whack her with the branch. That, however, was when it all started to go wrong and things began spinning out of control. As soon as you killed Joan, the beech tree, weakened by the storm, finally collapsed. Must have scared you rigid – lots of noise as it came crashing down – and

220

it landed right beside your car. Now you knew you had to move fast. Somebody might come to investigate and cars would start backing up sooner rather than later. Then one of you had a brainwave. Before anyone else showed up, you arranged Joan's body under the tree to make it look like she had died in an accident.

'No,' Carstairs sobbed and started to cry. 'You've got it all wrong. We found Joan there under the tree when we got there!'

'No, you didn't, Mary,' Agatha said. 'It took me a while to figure out what didn't quite work with your story and the crime scene . . . and it was Anthony's car. Your car was parked in the lay-by nose-to-nose with Joan's car, but you couldn't have parked there like that after the tree fell. You were seen driving down towards Ancombe Vale, but you couldn't have got past the tree if it had been across the road. You were parked on the wrong side of the tree!'

Carstairs and Feldrake exchanged looks and Agatha continued.

'I'm now in no doubt that Stella realised that, too. Like me, it took her a little while but she worked it out before I did. By the time she got there, there were other people, plenty of witnesses, so you had to abandon your plan for a double murder. Yet the opportunity to get rid of Stella later presented itself quite unexpectedly, didn't it?

'You see, on the day I ended up in the river, we all went down to the woods for the same reason: we were all looking for Joan's phone. Stella had discovered that the warbler message was fake. You told everyone that Joan was in the woods looking for the magnolia warbler and

221

Stella's competitive nature started to make her wonder why Joan got to the woods before she did. Who would want to send them on a wild warbler chase anyway, and why? That's when she realised your car was in the wrong place and the timings were all wrong. She knew that taking a look at Joan's phone would shed some light on that.'

'Actually,' Bill chimed in, 'Miss Smart phoned me to ask if she could take a look at Miss Feldrake's phone. I told her we hadn't recovered any phone from the scene.'

'That meant either you had it, Anthony, or it was still there,' Agatha went on. 'So Stella went to search for it. When you and Mary didn't receive the phone from the police along with Joan's other personal effects, you also figured out it must still be in the woods, where she dropped it.'

'You were looking for the phone when we saw you there, Miss Carstairs,' Roy said.

'And so were you, Anthony,' Agatha added.

'Ridiculous!' Feldrake blurted. 'I was here in Tweeting Bottom all day!'

'No, you weren't,' Toni said. 'When I called round here that day, there was nobody home.'

'You were out there in the woods, Anthony,' said Agatha. 'When Mary made her way back to the road and I spotted Stella's body in the river, you were watching. You came up behind me, shoved me in on top of her, then ran away and hid, watching me drowning in the river!'

'I've heard enough,' Bill said, producing two sets of handcuffs. 'Remember how to use these, John?' He handed one set of cuffs to John and pointed to Mary Carstairs.

'It's something I'll never forget,' John said. 'Let me have your hands, please, Miss Carstairs.'

John stepped towards Carstairs and Bill turned to Feldrake, whose eyes were wide with panic. Suddenly, showing what Agatha thought was a startling display of agility, Feldrake vaulted the coffee table in the middle of the room and grabbed Roy, flinging him aside. Roy staggered backwards, slamming into Bill who was knocked off balance. Feldrake lunged towards the door and Agatha stretched out a leg, aiming a swift kick at his ankle. Feldrake squealed, stumbled, but kept his footing and limped off at a surprising rate to the kitchen. With Agatha on his tail, he reached the back door, hobbled outside and slammed the door in her face. He was halfway down the lawn when Patrick stepped out from behind the bird hide. Feldrake paused and Patrick raised his fists.

'An old fart like me wouldn't be much use mixing it with youngsters these days,' Patrick growled, 'but I fancy my chances against another old fart like you.'

Feldrake let out a roar, ready to charge, then was felled by what felt like a cannon ball hitting him in the back. He was flat on his face with Agatha sitting on his back pummelling his head and shoulders with her clenched fists.

'That'll do, Agatha,' John said, gently hoisting her to her feet while Bill handcuffed Feldrake.

'I was looking forward to having a shot at him,' Patrick said, disappointed.

223

'No, Patrick,' Agatha puffed, breathing hard and pushing a few stray hairs from her face. 'That swine tried to kill me. He was all mine.'

Bill took Feldrake out to where Carstairs was being loaded into a police car by his people and John stood by the car, chatting with some of the officers he knew. Agatha and Toni left the Feldrake house and walked round to knock on the Bellinghams' door. When it was opened, both Mr and Mrs Bellingham were standing there.

'What on earth's going on out here?' Mrs Bellingham asked, both of them looking out at the police cars and police officers, with more arriving as they watched.

Agatha explained everything and fished Joan Feldrake's phone out of her handbag.

'I assume you recognise this,' she said, holding it up. Mrs Bellingham started to bluster. 'No need to say anything,' Agatha continued. 'There are photographs on here that I'm sure you'd rather no one else saw. I don't think Joan Feldrake was much of a blackmailer. I don't think she made any copies of the photos. Had she done so, you'd probably have found them when you searched her place.'

The Bellinghams looked at each other in alarm.

'I have to hand this over to the police as evidence in a murder case,' Agatha said, 'but before I do, I'm going to give it to a young man who works for me. He's a bit of a whizz with these things.'

'Best not tell him that,' Toni said, imagining Simon's face. 'He's cocky enough as it is.'

'Some say you can never really delete files completely from a device like this,' Agatha said, 'but our guy can. By the time this goes to the police, the photos will have disappeared. No one will ever see them again.'

A wave of relief swept over the Bellinghams' faces.

'Thank you, Mrs Raisin,' Mrs Bellingham said, reaching out to shake Agatha's hand.

'You're welcome, Mrs Bellingham,' Agatha replied. 'Enjoy your holiday.'

Over the next couple of weeks, things began to return to normal. There was a huge amount of form filling to be done and an avalanche of questions to be answered at Mircester Police Station but, thankfully, Wilkes kept his distance from all of that. Agatha even had the satisfaction of seeing another Charlotte Clark headline in the *Mircester Telegraph*: 'Private Eye Cleared after Police Blunder'.

Agatha was interviewed extensively in the report, her favourite quote being: 'I always enjoy working with Mircester Police. The vast majority of them are hard-working officers doing a difficult and dangerous job. They are the salt of the earth. Sadly the same can't always be said of certain higher ranks.'

She showed the same dignity and restraint when she was interviewed by a clutch of TV reporters, using every second of her time in the spotlight to promote herself and Raisin Investigations as a reliable, trustworthy professional outfit. Then, as suddenly as her media star had risen, it swiftly expired, the newshounds scuttling off in search of the next big story. Following her flash of fame, however, business was booming as never before.

John was excited to be going back aboard ship as a senior member of the cruise line's entertainment staff and resident dance instructor. Because he was excited, Agatha was excited for him. She knew she was going to miss him terribly, but consoled herself with the fact that he would only be gone for a couple of weeks. A few days before he was due to leave, she arrived at his house where they planned to use his garden dance studio to, as John put it, 'sharpen up his twinkle toes'. Then there would be dinner at the Italian restaurant and more dancing followed by . . . whatever led on from that.

Agatha parked in John's driveway, walked over to ring the doorbell and stood for a few seconds on the doorstep but heard no sound of movement from the house. Then she smiled to herself. Of course! John would be out in the back garden, in the studio. She slipped through the gate at the side of the house and skipped along the paving stones set into the lawn. She stepped into the studio just as Frank Sinatra's 'Fly Me to the Moon' finished with a flourish and saw John sitting peacefully in a corner beside a table on which sat a bottle of champagne and two glasses. She swished across the floor as a ripple of piano announced Nat King Cole's 'Let There Be Love' and looked down at John to see his eyes were closed. He had a faint smile on his face. He looked happy and relaxed. He was asleep.

'Come on, sleepyhead!' she called, standing on the dance floor in front of him and holding out her hands. 'I don't want to miss this one!'

John didn't move. Stepping forward, she leaned over to shake his shoulder but got no reaction.

'John!' she cried. 'John! Wake up!'

She touched his face and it felt cold. Panic rising in her stomach, she held her fingers to his neck but could find no pulse. John wasn't going to wake up.

'No . . .' she breathed, feeling her legs buckle, as though all her strength had seeped out through the floor. She slumped down beside his chair, held his hand and rested her head on his arm, staring across the dance floor, letting the music play out. She then picked up her phone, dialled and quietly said, 'I need to report a sudden death.'

The paramedics who arrived told her it looked like a heart attack. The doctors who later spoke to her told her John had a previously undiagnosed left ventricular systolic dysfunction that had undoubtedly been present for a long while and could have caused the heart attack at any time over the last few months. None of that really mattered. It didn't change anything. John was still gone.

Agatha stayed away from the office for a while, although Toni called her most days to check that she was okay and to assure her that everything at work was running smoothly. Between them, Toni and Margaret Bloxby made most of the funeral arrangements. Agatha seemed peculiarly detached. Even over the phone Toni could sense a subdued, flat atmosphere at the cottage in Lilac

Lane, and those who came across Agatha strolling through Carsely saw a beautifully dressed, immaculately made-up version of Agatha Raisin with a distracted, distant look in her eyes. She always acknowledged a 'good morning' but never smiled or stopped to talk to anyone. So it continued until the day of the funeral.

That morning, Toni phoned to check the schedule with Agatha to make sure she knew precisely when she would be calling round to go with her to St Jude's. Normally she'd have expected some sort of backlash, Agatha never usually tolerating anyone attempting to remind her what she should be doing or when she should be doing it. Reminders like that simply weren't normally necessary with Agatha Raisin. This situation, however, was far from normal.

For Agatha, the day began much like most others recently. She rose a little later than was her habit, led the cats downstairs to be fed and sat at the kitchen table with a cup of coffee listening to the radio. Not so long ago, she mused, she'd have started today by lighting up a cigarette to smoke with coffee. In fact, a day like this would have required more than one cigarette. It would have needed . . . she didn't know how many. There had never been a day like this and, in any case, she had long since decided that she could handle everything just as well without a nicotine hit. She could handle this day. It wasn't a day she had been looking forward to, but it was an ordeal she would face up to, and for which she had laid her own plans. Today, she had decided, was to be the beginning of the rest of her life and she was going to do things her way.

Having showered, done her hair and taken special care over her make-up, she stood in front of the full-length mirror in her bedroom making sure that her dress was exactly as she wanted it. She remembered when she had first worn it, having dieted furiously and exercised herself half to death to make sure her stomach was the flattest it had been in years. Now, the dress fitted better than ever. It was almost time. Everything would be fine. She walked downstairs to the kitchen and opened the fridge to retrieve her handbag.

Toni, Roy and James, recently returned from Iceland, stood at Agatha's garden gate. A black stretch limousine and a hearse waited in the high street, each too long to be able to turn round in Lilac Lane.

'How has she been?' Roy asked, looking a little nervous and most unlike himself, devoid of all ostentation in a sober black suit.

'I've hardly seen her, old boy,' James replied, 'and whenever I have she's simply said she's fine and that she'd rather not talk.'

'It's not just that she's not talking,' Toni said, her voice full of concern for her friend. 'She's not doing anything. There's no emotion. She hasn't even lost her temper!'

'That's not good,' said Roy. 'She can conjure up a temper like you wouldn't believe in the blink of an eye.'

'Oh, we'd believe, all right,' James said. 'We've all seen it.'

'The worst thing is,' Toni said, 'she hasn't cried. Nobody's seen her shed even one tear. I know the police officers who were there at John's place – they have to attend a sudden death to make sure everything's above board – and they said she didn't even cry then, when she'd just found John.'

'It's not normal, is it?' said James.

'When did "normal" ever apply to Agatha Raisin?' Roy shrugged.

Toni walked up the garden path and rang the doorbell, Agatha opening the door straight away, ready to go.

'Hi, Agatha,' Toni began, 'it's time to ... um ... Are you sure about this?'

Toni stared, her mouth hanging open, at Agatha's dress. It was a pale peach, off-the-shoulder gown with a tight bodice and a skirt that flared from the waist down to the calf-length hem from where an open frill ran back up to her hip. A diamond pendant hung around her neck, with matching earrings and a diamond bracelet that dazzled in the sunshine.

'You mean my dress?' Agatha asked. 'I could say the same about you. I've never seen quite such a demure little black dress. It makes you look far too skinny and it's put years on you.'

Toni froze for a second. That actually sounded a lot more like the old Agatha. The question was, did today call for this particular brand of Raisin? She steeled herself, deciding they simply had to move ahead.

'The cars are ready at the end of the lane to take us to the church,' she said.

'I'm not going in one of those bloody things,' Agatha said, peering down towards the high street. 'My ride will be here any second.'

Then came the roar and rattle of a clattering diesel engine and a brilliant red tractor festooned with white and pink flowers wheeled into Lilac Lane, occasional puffs of smoke escaping from the funnel-like exhaust. Gethin Fawkes rumbled up to Agatha's cottage, swung the Cropmaster round and stood up at the wheel.

'Your chariot awaits, madam!' he called and Agatha smiled.

'You lot can ride in those black monstrosities if you like,' she said. 'I'm arriving in style!'

'Agatha, I . . .' Toni put an uncertain hand on her boss's arm as Agatha went to move past her.

'It's all right, Toni,' Agatha said. She smiled and squeezed Toni's hand. 'Everything's going to be fine.'

Gethin, dressed in black trousers, a black waistcoat and a white shirt with a grey flat cap, jumped down to help and ultimately partly lift Agatha up into her seat, the Cropmaster never having been designed to be accessed by someone wearing such a dress or such vertiginously high heels.

The tractor led the black cars up the high street to the church, where Gethin cut the engine, dismounted and helped Agatha down as elegantly as possible. The noise of the tractor engine had scarcely receded when the tinkle of tiny bells could be heard. A group of Morris dancers appeared from the direction of the church hall, skipping along the street, the bands of bells around their knees sprinkling a rhythm while they danced around the hearse. They formed two lines, clashed the sticks they were carrying and wove an intricate pattern of steps around each other before disappearing back towards the church hall.

231

Gethin then started up the Cropmaster again and drove off, disappearing back down the high street. Six police officers in full dress uniform and white gloves marched to the hearse to carry the coffin. Agatha made her way into the church while the coffin was unloaded and was met by a small group of John's friends and colleagues, including Bill and Alice Wong, who both gave her glorious smiles. Alice leaned over to whisper in Agatha's ear.

'I'd recognise that dress anywhere,' she said. 'Good for you!'

Also standing in line was Detective Chief Inspector Wilkes, not in his customary shabby suit, but in dress uniform, shining pips on his shoulders.

'I'm ... um ... sorry for your loss, Mrs Raisin,' he mumbled, looking off to her left.

Agatha stopped and stared straight in his face until he was forced to make eye contact.

'He hated you,' was all she said.

The church was full. Making her way to the front pew, Agatha recognised most of those present, although some of John's former work friends were strangers to her. The coffin was brought in, decked in flowers, and set on a table to one side, draped in purple velvet. The rest of the proceedings passed in a blur as far as Agatha was concerned. There were hymns, some standing up and sitting back down, a reading of some sort and a monologue of some description from the Reverend Bloxby before he finally looked over the lectern behind which he was standing and nodded to Agatha.

'And now I believe Mrs Raisin would like to say a few

words,' he announced before leaving the lectern and moving soundlessly across the stone floor to sit down beside Margaret.

Agatha stood, hung her handbag over her left arm and marched to the lectern, her high heels clacking like pistol shots on the floor. She stood behind the lectern, resisting the temptation to lean her elbows on its sloping surface for support. She noted that it had a narrow flat surface at the front. That would be handy.

'John would be pleased that so many of you have made the effort to be here today,' she said, feeling a knot in her throat and a slight wobble in her voice. That wouldn't do. She got angry with herself, angry with her voice, and that sorted it out. Now she was back in control. 'He would be pleased, but I'm not. I'm not pleased that you're here. I'm not pleased that I'm here. I'm not pleased that any of us are here. We shouldn't have to be here! John should still be with us, and it makes me so angry that—'

She stopped and took a few deep breaths, her fists clenched on the lectern.

'But I promised him that's not how it would be. I didn't get to say goodbye to him and I didn't come here to say goodbye, either. I came to celebrate. Those Morris dancers some of you saw outside were John's friends. He danced with them. He didn't do that for any kind of payment or prestige. He did it for the fun, and the beer . . . and to celebrate. John and I always had plenty to celebrate. There's nothing like dancing for a good celebration.

'We talked about getting married, you know. Not for

very long. It wasn't what either of us wanted. We just wanted each other, and that's the way we decided to go. We would each have our own space, we would have our separate lives, and we would have our life together. We would have our cake and eat it. That way, all the time we spent together would be special, and it was, and I'm here to celebrate that.

'Those of you who know me will be surprised to hear me baring my soul in public. It's not something I do, but today is different. Today is for John . . .'

As she was talking, her voice faltered a little again, her eyes moistened and a tear rolled down her cheek. She let it go. People would see her crying. She didn't care. Her waterproof mascara might not hold. She didn't care.

'Those of you who've never seen me cry before – and that's pretty much all of you – lap it up. You'll never see this again. Some of you might not think I'm dressed for a funeral. Well, I looked at the black dresses in my wardrobe and they might be fine for a fancy dinner or a cocktail party but not for a celebration – and this is a celebration.'

She opened her handbag. It looked for all the world like she was searching for a tissue, but instead she produced a champagne glass, followed by a small, airline-sized bottle of champagne. She filled the glass and set it down in front of her on the level strip at the front of the lectern.

'So I'm not wearing black. I'm wearing a dress I've had for quite some time. This is the dress I wore to the wedding of Alice and Bill Wong. It was there that I first danced with a man I hardly knew – John Glass. That was a special moment. That's one worth celebrating.'

She couldn't stop the tears that were now streaming down her face, but she held her voice steady.

'He was the best partner I ever danced with. He was the best thing that ever happened to me. He was . . . just the best. He'd love it that I'm wearing this dress. This is me and he told me he loved me just as I am and . . . and I loved him. I always will.

'But there will be no endless mourning. There will be no wasted years. We promised each other that. So I will go on. Agatha Raisin will go on. Raisin Investigations will go on. Life for all of us will go on and John will remain a part of us. I'll remember him every day, and I'll be happy because I will celebrate every memory.'

She reached for the glass and raised it high.

'There's a box over there with a body in it, but that's not John. My John is long gone. My John is out there dancing in the stars, the brightest of them all. Now that's definitely worth celebrating! Here's to us, John!'

She took a small sip from the glass, then put it gently back on the lectern. For a moment, there was complete silence, then came the sound of one person clapping. Toni got to her feet, her face wet with tears. She was the one clapping. Then Roy stood next to her, also clapping, and the whole Raisin Investigations team were on their feet an instant later applauding. Sir Charles Fraith stood and was immediately obscured when the row of uniformed officers in front of him got to their feet, clapping enthusiastically. One of them stopped for second and wiped away a tear with his white glove.

'Champagne in church . . . applause at a funeral,' the Reverend Bloxby said to his wife. 'It's all most improper—'

'Not today, Alf,' Margaret said, already out of her seat. 'Now stand up.'

With the applause ringing around the church, Agatha looked out over everyone in the congregation. The applause wasn't for her. They were celebrating John, and that was what she wanted. She stepped out from behind the lectern, walked slowly down the aisle to the church door and out into Carsely High Street. She then turned towards Lilac Lane and walked home alone.